TWISTED VOW

SINFUL TRUTHS BOOK 2

ELLA MILES

FREE BOOKS

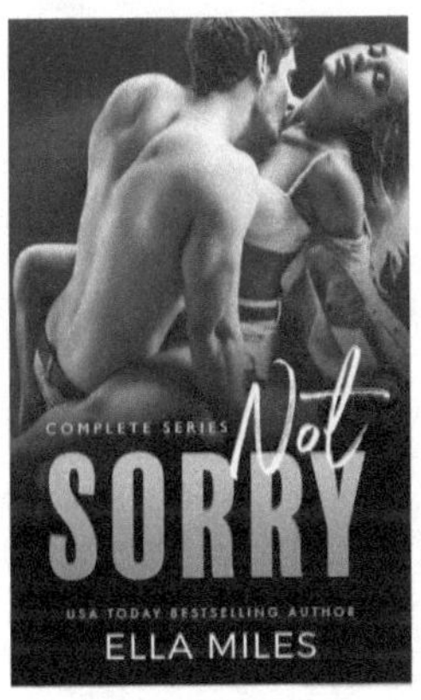

Read **Not Sorry** for **FREE!** And sign up to get my latest releases & updates here→EllaMiles.com/freebooks

Follow me on BookBub to get notified of my new releases→Follow on BookBub Here

Join Ella's Bellas FB group to grab my **FREE** book **Pretend I'm Yours**→Join Ella's Bellas Here

TRUTH OR LIES WORLD

TRUTH OR LIES SERIES:

Taken by Lies #1
Betrayed by Truths #2
Trapped by Lies #3
Stolen by Truths #4
Possessed by Lies #5
Consumed by Truths #6

SINFUL TRUTHS SERIES:

Sinful Truth #1
Twisted Vow #2
Reckless Fall #3
Tangled Promise #4
Fallen Love #5
Broken Anchor #6

1
———

SIREN

I'M NOT the one in need of saving.

I repeat those words over and over to myself.

They are true.

I never speak a lie. Or even think one.

I chose this life.

I was given an option, all those years ago, and this is the life I chose for myself. I chose to work for Julian Reed. I chose to take down dangerous men. I chose to live my life on the edge of right and wrong. I chose to use my body as a weapon.

And I enjoy what I do.

I may hate my boss—Julian Reed.

But I love hurting men more.

Men have done nothing but hurt me. Men promise me the world. They promise me their love. They promise me their fidelity.

Ha.

No man can ever keep his promises. No man's heart is truly pure. No man can keep his dick in his pants when he's faced with a flirty woman, even when he wears a ring around his fourth finger.

Every man deserves exactly what he gets from me. And Zeke is no different.

Zeke Kane—I didn't know his name, not until he spilled his secrets. Not until I learned he works for the infamous Mr. Black. Rumor is the former Mr. Black died a few years back. And there is a war raging for the new heir of the throne of one of the most notorious crime organizations in the world. Mr. Black has his hand in everything. So Julian taking him down would make him one of the most powerful men in the world.

I'm sitting crooked in the chair in Julian's living room as I type on my laptop. And have been for the last few hours.

Ever since I accomplished my mission—getting Zeke to spill his boss to me—I've been searching for everything I can find about Zeke and his former boss.

I click on a grainy picture. Two men of similar age stand next to Zeke. Zeke and a blonde man flank the man in the middle, who must be the new Mr. Black.

My heart thumps in strange patterns as my eyes skim from each man, and lastly, land on Zeke. He's wearing his classic outfit of dark jeans and a black T-shirt. But in this picture, his hair is down. He looks grizzly and bulky and so fucking handsome.

I snap the laptop closed as I feel my cheeks heat.

Nope, not happening. I can't be lusting over the man I just locked up in the basement of his house.

Right now, there are at least three guards watching Zeke. I don't need to be thinking about him. I need to be thinking about the next mission Julian is going to give me.

I've worked with Julian long enough to know what he's going to say before he even says it.

"Good job, pet," Julian says as he enters the living room with two scotches in hand.

He hands me one, then grips my shoulder in a congratulatory way.

I snarl. "I think you can stop calling me 'pet' now."

Julian smirks as he sits down on the couch opposite me and crosses his lower leg over his knee in the way only men do. He sips his scotch, staring me down.

"Why? I like the nickname. It's been years since I called you that. Since the night you broke into my house and we came to an arrangement."

I sip on the scotch, staring Julian down in equal measure. "My name is Aria; I suggest you use it."

"Well, that's not any fun. You let Zeke call you all sorts of fun names—Siren."

I narrow my eyes.

He chuckles. "Siren was the perfect name for you. What I love even more is that you told him exactly who you were with one word, and he was too stupid to realize his own mistake."

I feel agitation rise in my chest, but I don't take the bait.

I've always felt that breaking into Julian's house was my worst mistake and my strongest moment. That night, years ago, changed my life in ways I can't describe. Ways that are too painful to relive right now...

But what I did to Zeke feels exactly the same—I hurt him. I outsmarted and overpowered a built man. I feel strong, yet everything I did was painful. *What if Zeke is the one man who doesn't deserve what I did to him?*

Sure, he's a man, and he deserves to pay for mankind's sins. *But what if he truly isn't a sinner?*

What if I made a mistake? He said he didn't sell those

women. *What did he do with them then? How did Julian get his money if Zeke didn't sell them?*

I down the rest of my drink, needing to forget about Zeke at least for tonight, and alcohol will help me do that.

Julian smiles and downs his scotch. He refills his drink at the bar cart in the corner of the room and brings the remainder of the bottle to fill my glass.

He sets the bottle on the coffee table between us. His eyes blaze as he looks up and down my body. I'm still wearing nothing but a robe. I know how badly Julian wants me, he's made his feelings perfectly clear several times before. But that doesn't mean he will ever get me.

I don't tighten the sash to cover up more of my skin. Julian may be my boss, he may control my life, but I control him too. And I won't relinquish any of my power.

Julian holds up his glass. "To you."

I hold up mine as well, and we clink our glasses together before returning to drinking.

"I mean it. I think this is your best work yet, Aria."

I nod, *it is my best work.* Usually, it doesn't take this much effort to get a man to spill his secrets. A lap dance. A little too much to drink. A slip of my hand on his thigh.

But I knew from the moment I met Zeke that he was different. He would require more. And my suspicions were proven right.

"Your idea to pretend you were being sold to see if Zeke would take the bait and try and save you was incredible. I truly believed that you thought you were being sold," Julian says.

I stare down at the scotch in my glass, those feelings coming back to me. "That's because if my plan failed, if Zeke didn't buy me, I *would* have been sold."

Julian stills.

"You wouldn't have saved me. You would have let a man buy me," I say, my words full of hate.

Julian shrugs. "I would have."

I shake my head, my anger spilling out of me. "You're an asshole."

He chuckles. "You already knew that." He sets his glass down on the table and leans forward. "But, you know why I would have let you be sold to any man?"

"Why?"

"Because you don't need me or any man to save you." He pats my thigh as he says it.

He's right. I don't need a man to save me. I always save myself before any man has a chance to save me.

But his words don't stop me from being mad. Yes, if I had been sold to another man, I would have shot him dead and escaped before he had a chance to touch me, but that doesn't absolve Julian of his other sins.

"Why did you do it?" I ask, my voice trembling as I say it. This time, I wrap my robe tight around my body, ensuring Julian can't see any of my skin.

He falls back in his chair, seeming to choose his words carefully. He doesn't have to ask for clarification on what I'm asking. He knows. Because we had an agreement, and he broke it.

"Zeke needed motivation," he answers.

"No! I was handling him!" I snap back.

"And I was tired of waiting. So I just provided a little push."

I take a deep breath in and out, so I don't kill Julian right now and ruin everything I've been working so hard on for the past four years.

"You had me tied up and dragged in front of a room of

strangers," I say calmly with my eyes closed, reliving one of the worst nights of my life.

"You had me manhandled upstairs to your bedroom," I open my eyes, needing Julian to see exactly what he did to me.

My eyes burn red and tears water the corner, ready to spill free.

"You ripped the clothes from my body."

I have to look away for a second as the tears spill, and my body shakes with rage. I exhale deeply, letting it all out before I face Julian again.

"You spit alcohol into my eyes—I could have gone blind.

"You hit me, kicked me—I could have died."

The last part is the hardest. But he needs to hear every fucking word of the pain he caused me. Not that he cares, Julian Reed doesn't have a heart. I learned that a long time ago. It's one of the reasons I'm in this situation to begin with.

"You pulled out your cock. You shoved it between my thighs. And if Zeke hadn't shown up, you would have raped me." My body may tremble, but my voice is strong. I spit every word out. Every drop of pain and fear I felt that night.

I'm a tough, skilled woman. I know how to get out of most situations. I know how to save myself. But I couldn't save myself that night. I signed a contract with Julian years ago. If I had fought back, I would have broken the contract, and I would have lost everything I've worked so hard for.

Julian knew that. He knew I was defenseless, which is why he attacked me. Because he wanted to, not because he wanted to push Zeke into spilling—I was close to doing that on my own. In fact, Julian's little stunt almost killed me and probably delayed Zeke telling me the truth.

"You made me depend on a man to save me," I growl.

"I did," Julian says, not backing down.

I want to punch him, kick his ass for what he did to me. But like I said, I signed a contract—one that I have no hope of getting out of, at least not like this. If I lay a finger on Julian, I lose—*every-fucking-thing.*

He knows I won't touch him.

"Never again," I say.

Julian shakes his head. "No, you said your peace, now it's my turn. You work for me, Aria. Me! You made your decision, now live with it. And when I decide to deviate from our original plan, you don't fight me on it, and you don't get to lecture me. If you do it again, there will be consequences. Understand?"

Julian's voice is full of threats, but they aren't empty warnings—they are real. And his punishments hurt worse than anything any other man could ever inflict on me, because Julian knows me better than anyone else. He knows my weak points, and he knows where to push to deliver the most pain.

So as much as I want to argue back, as much as I need Julian to promise never to lay a finger on me again—I can't.

Instead, I down more of the scotch. I need it in order to sleep tonight. But it sure as hell won't be under Julian's roof. I'll go take one of the small boats out and sleep on the water. I'll feel safer that way—sleeping out under the stars, rocking along with the waves.

I grab the bottle of scotch and pour myself another glass, while I stare Julian down, letting him know everything I think and feel with my eyes, since I can't say them with my words.

I hate him.

"I'm going to bed," I say, downing the glass of expensive scotch meant to be enjoyed slowly, not chugged like a shot of cheap tequila.

"You know what your next task is?" Julian asks.

I stand and set the glass down on the table. "I already used all the power I have against Zeke. He no longer cares about me. He doesn't even like me. In fact, I'm pretty sure he hates me. There is nothing I can do to convince him to turn on his boss. You are going to have to do that on your own. I did my job."

I turn, intending to walk the fuck out.

"Your job isn't finished until I say it is, Aria."

I stop. I take it back; it's not only 'pet' that I hate him calling me. I also hate it when he calls me Aria, Siren, and any name really. I hate it all.

Julian walks up behind me and runs his hand through my hair, brushing it over one side of my shoulders, exposing my neck so he can stroke it.

"You're right, Zeke hates you. Use his hate then."

I swallow hard, refusing to cry any more in front of Julian. But I can do the task Julian gave me, just like I do every other task.

Use Zeke's hate—that I can do. I strut away from Julian. I know a little something about hate.

2

ZEKE

It's been a week.

A fucking week.

I've been locked up in this cell under the house I rent from Julian for a week.

The bars hold me in the filthy basement, but they aren't what concern me. With enough willpower and strength, both which I have, I could break the bars within minutes.

But once I escape from my cell, I have guards to take out —three to be exact.

Again, not a problem. Even though they are armed, and I'm not. I could take on a hundred men by myself.

Escaping is the easy part. The hard part is ensuring my friends are safe. Julian knows who my boss is. And he wants him. He wants to use me to get what he wants from Enzo Black; I just don't know what that is exactly. *Does Julian want his power? His empire? His status? Or is there something more about the Black empire that I'm not aware of?*

The bars and guards aren't holding me in this cell, my need to protect my boss and friends is. If I run without killing Julian first, they will never be safe, even if I never return to them. And they're my family. I grew up with Enzo and Langston—I consider them brothers.

Why didn't I kill Julian when I had the chance? I didn't owe him a damn thing.

Because I'm an idiot, that's why.

An idiot who fell for a siren.

No, that can't be true. I didn't fall for her. At least, I didn't fall in love. I just fell under her spell. I let her manipulate me. I let her use her body and my need to protect the innocent against me.

Except Siren isn't innocent.

So I shouldn't want to protect her, except... *Fuck*, I have no idea what I want anymore when it comes to that woman.

Do I want to destroy her like I do Julian?

Do I want to punish her for what she did to me and for putting my family in danger?

Do I want to fuck her hard against a brick wall?

What. Do. I. Want?

I run my hand through my long hair. I really wish I had a scrunchie to tie my hair up with because it's driving me crazy right now.

No—focus. I need to protect my family—Enzo, Kai, Langston, Liesel.

I need to write a letter. I need to send something to warn them while ensuring Julian doesn't find out where they are.

If I call, he could track them.

But a letter that's not even written to them...that could save them.

That's my new goal, to convince the guards to give me a pen and paper to write on. Should be easy enough. The guards have already brought me food, books, a new pillow and blanket, and even whiskey. They don't care what I do as long as I stay locked up in the cell. Apparently, Julian and

Siren haven't decided how to get me to break—to give up Mr. Black. They don't realize I'd rather die a thousand times than give them even one shred of information that could cause harm to my family. I've spent my entire life protecting them. I've sacrificed my life before to keep them safe; I'll do it again.

And again and again and again.

I hear the door open to the basement stairs.

My guard, Pete, who is sitting across from me, looks at his watch. He's been sitting reading a newspaper like it's the 1950s or something. It must be time for a guard change.

He stands up, ready to vacate his seat for his replacement.

My guards have mostly rotated between the same three men. Occasionally, a new guard works into the mix. But it should be Frank who takes over, unless there has been a change or it's his day off.

But when I hear the click, click, click of the footsteps on the stairs, I know there has been a change in the guard schedule, and not a good one.

"Thank you, Pete. I got it from here," Siren says.

I refuse to look at her. I'm lying on the makeshift bed I made on the floor with the pillows and blankets the guards have been bringing me. I have a book opened on my stomach, and I pretend to read.

Ignore her.

She doesn't get to see how angry she's made me. And I sure as hell won't fall for any more of her tricks.

"So that's how it's going to be? You aren't even going to look at me?" she asks in her snarky, annoying voice. I can't believe I didn't realize how annoying her voice was before— *that's because it's not annoying, not even now.*

Focus—read the words in my book. But all I see is blah, blah, blah on the page.

"We tracked down your friends. Their yacht is off the shores of Greece," she says.

I growl and finally look up at her.

She's standing in a tight black dress, sharp heels, and red lipstick. Her dress cuts down in the front, revealing her ample cleavage, and she's not wearing a bra, so her nipples point sharply at me. At least they do until she folds her arms in front of her chest and sways her hips to the side.

"You're lying," I say.

"Am I? I don't lie."

"No, you don't. That is the only honest thing about you. But your words weren't sharp, you're biting your lip, and your heart rate has picked up. You're lying."

She unfolds her arms. "Does it matter if I was lying? I got you to talk to me, so mission accomplished." She smiles and gives me a wink.

I shake my head in annoyance. *How can I keep letting her get under my skin?* I try to go back to my book, but I know it's no use.

"Why are you here?" I ask.

She licks her lips, and then walks back and takes a seat in the chair. She crosses her legs, and as she does, her dress rises higher up her thighs.

She wore the dress to taunt me—*don't fall for it.*

"For you to yell at me," she answers.

I frown. "What?"

I try to figure out her angle. *Why would she come here so I could yell at her? What game is she playing now?*

"You heard me. Now bring it. Yell at me like you want to. You'll feel better," she says, motioning for me to bring it on with a wave of her hand.

I stand up, my anger getting the best of me. "I don't want to get it out. I want to harness my anger into giving you everything you deserve."

She tilts her head. "You sure you don't want to yell at me, Zeke Kane?"

A low rumble of a growl escapes. She knows my last name. Which means she has done her research. She has looked up Enzo and possibly Kai. And every other person who works for Enzo. She could have been telling the truth when she said she knew where their yacht is right now.

I take a step backward, realizing how stupid I was to tell her my secret. Even if I thought we were starting something incredible together. Even if I thought she could turn into the love of my life, I should have never trusted her. I should have never spoken a word about Enzo Black. I should have protected him with my life like I vowed to do all those years ago.

"You weren't lying, were you?" I ask.

She raises an eyebrow. "We don't know Mr. Black's exact location, but we will soon enough."

I frown.

"Now, are you ready to take me up on my offer of yelling at me?" she asks.

No, because who I really want to yell at is myself.

I grab the bars and shake them; the metal of the bars rattles, but otherwise, they don't budge.

She jumps at my outburst.

I'm the strong, quiet type. I don't let my emotions get the best of me. But with her, I'm all emotion.

She takes a deep breath and then leans forward in her chair. "You would have done the same thing if you were in my shoes, Zeke."

I feel like she just slapped me, punched me in the gut,

threw me from a moving car. Because if that is what she really thinks, she didn't learn a thing about me in our time together.

"No, I wouldn't have. I'm not a monster!" my voice ricochets off the brick walls, and I watch her heart thump wildly against her chest. I can be terrifying when I want to be. My physical size alone makes me scary, but then when you pair it with my deep, intimidating voice and my bursting muscles, I become a beast. That's what Siren called me—a beast. But it's clear she really thinks of me as a monster.

I pant my breaths in and out, still gripping the bars. Bars I could bend with my bare hands. *But then what? Could I really hurt her?*

Yes.

No.

Fuck.

I study her closer, and I can no longer tell why her body is trembling, her heart speeding, her breath catching. *Why are her lips parting, her tongue resting on the edge of her plump bottom lip, and her eyes growing big? Is she afraid of me? Or is she turned on? Or maybe it's all an act?*

I decide it's option number three. She's a better actor than she initially let on. It has to be. If she works for Julian, then she isn't afraid of any man. Especially one locked behind bars. And there is no way she's turned on by me, not when she thinks I'm a twisted monster. She's just acting so she can learn more secrets from me.

She stands up and flips her hair in that seductive way all women know how to do—tossing it sexily over her shoulder. Her eyes lock with mine.

Don't get drawn into her! Don't let her draw you back under her spell. She's a siren, remember.

She keeps walking, not stopping until her face is inches from mine.

I could reach out and grab her. Strangle her with my bare hands. Or bash her head against the bars. I could knock her out and search her body for a weapon, key, or cell phone—something that would help me get out of here.

But I don't.

I can't.

And my siren, knows it.

It's why she isn't scared of me even though I'm bigger and stronger than she is. Yes, she manipulated me into this cage. Yes, she used her physical skills against me. But the only reason she won is because I was in too much shock to fight back.

Siren grabs the bars, just below where I'm holding them. Our breaths mix together in the space between us. And my body can't decide between choking her and kissing her.

Goddammit, why do I have to be such a man? And why does she have to be so beautifully feminine?

If she were a man, I wouldn't hesitate. I would knock her out in seconds.

No—it's not that she's a woman. It's that she's her—Siren, strong, fierce, and a woman I wanted to protect. My feelings can't change for her in an instant. It takes time. I'm pissed, but it doesn't stop me from lusting after her. Especially when I never got to sink my cock inside her.

I want nothing more than to fuck her hard, fast, and uncontrollably against every rough surface I can find—the wall, the dining room table, the hood of my car, the coarse sand.

"How do we take down Mr. Black?" she asks.

I don't blink; I don't move. If she thinks I will ever answer that question, she's an idiot. I would never betray my boss and friend. Enzo Black is one of only a handful of people I even consider my family.

She sighs, her head dropping slightly.

"You lost, Zeke. Don't make this any harder than it has to be," she whispers.

Our eyes meet again. "I'm not the one making this hard."

Her eyes flutter down; all this talk about making me hard makes her glance at my dick. And yes, it's fucking hard as a rock, but that's not what we are talking about.

I shake the bars again, and she comes back to reality. Her eyes resume her gaze on mine.

"Don't make me hurt you, Zeke."

"You already did."

"Save yourself. For once, put yourself above others."

"No, that's not who I am. I protect my friends, my family. I protect those who are innocent. I protect—that's who I am."

She cocks her head to the side, giving me a disappointed, scared for me look. So I deliver the final blow.

"I just shouldn't have protected *you*," I say.

Siren closes her eyes as my words sting her. But she's not Siren anymore; she's Aria. She's no longer in control. It doesn't matter that I'm in this cage, and she's out in the open. It doesn't matter that she manipulated me. My words hurt her. She's not the fierce woman willing to defy me; she's scared and wearing her heart on her sleeve.

I frown, narrowing my eyes as I study her, trying to remind myself that I thought she needed protecting before. She didn't. Whatever I'm seeing displayed on her body right now is a lie. It's not the truth. The only time she tells the truth is with her words, not her body. And her words are as much a riddle as they are the truth. *Remember that.*

Slowly, Siren walks away. She's a stranger to me now. She

stops at the base of the stairs. She turns and looks at me, her hand resting against the wall.

"Saving yourself will protect more than just you, Zeke," she says, and then she's gone.

Just like that, she's back to Siren. And I have no idea what to do with her parting words.

3

___

SIREN

I'M BEYOND FRUSTRATED.

It's been weeks, and I've made no progress on getting Zeke to spill his secrets. Julian is growing increasingly impatient with me. I'm running out of time before I have to deal with his wrath, but I'm no closer than I was weeks ago at getting Zeke to tell me anything about how to take down Mr. Black.

And finding Black's location on our own is futile. He travels too quickly in his yachts, going undetected through large spaces of water. By the time we find him, he's already moved on to a different location. And his home base of Miami would be harder to attack than on the ocean.

We could use Zeke as bait, lure him in by threatening Zeke's life. *But what if Mr. Black doesn't care about Zeke like Zeke cares about his boss?* Then all we would be doing is letting Black know that we have Zeke.

I sigh as I pace the main floor of Zeke's home. The furniture and decor are still ruined from when I threw my tantrum weeks ago.

I know what I have to attempt next, but I don't want to

do it. But I've tried everything else. I was nice and brought Zeke everything he could desire to keep him comfortable: good food, alcohol, books—I even brought a television down for him to watch. But none of those things got me any secrets. I tried bribing him with everything I brought too. But I just got a grumpy shoulder shrug for all of my troubles.

Bribing isn't the way to go.

I tried seducing him, using my body as bait, hoping he would spill a secret for a kiss, a blowjob, anything.

Nada.

That got me nowhere except my own flush red face when Zeke called me out for dressing like a slut. He looked me dead in the eye and swore he would never touch me again, let alone fuck me.

So today, I'm being myself. I'm wearing jeans and a tight-fitting black V-neck T-shirt. My hair is pulled up into a high ponytail. And I'm wearing makeup that makes me feel fierce, not slutty.

Because today I need all the strength I can get in order to take the next step with Zeke.

Joel, one of the guards, approaches me. "You ready?"

I nod.

"He's all yours then. He's in a foul mood. I doubt you are going to get any information out of him."

I look past Joel to the door to the basement. *Good, I'm glad Zeke is in a foul mood. Because I'm about to put him in a worse mood.*

I don't answer Joel. I just walk past him and descend the stairs.

Zeke is lying in his bed. Sometimes when I come downstairs, he's pacing or doing pushups or pull-ups. The pull-ups are my favorite—watching his biceps tense and curl his body up while he's shirtless is beyond sexy. But today he's lying on his bed staring up at the ceiling as he tosses a small ball up in the air.

I can tell from the creases on his forehead and the lost look in his eyes that he doesn't even notice my presence. He's in his own world. He's just as annoyed with this situation as I am.

I clear my throat. "Ready to talk today? Or are you going to keep wasting your life away in that cell?"

I already know his answer, but it doesn't keep me from asking every damn day, hoping he will answer me with even the smallest piece of information and put us both out of our misery.

Zeke's eyes cut to me. He chuckles to himself.

"What's so funny?" I ask.

"Tired of dressing like a whore, huh? Now you're going to try the tough, badass girl look?"

I look down at my outfit. I guess I wear my emotions on my body, but I'm just trying to prepare us both for what has to happen next.

"I guess so. You made it perfectly clear you don't find me attractive anymore, so why keep trying? Those dresses and heels weren't comfortable. I'd much rather wear jeans and boots."

He stares down at my boots. "Going to kick my ass with those boots? If so, you should make sure they have a metal toe; they will do more damage that way."

I hate how he can read me without saying anything. He knows I'm not here to play nice like I have every other day. Today, I'm here to hurt him. He can sense everything about me, which is why it was so surprising that my original plan worked; that I was able to trick him at all.

I didn't trick him, though. I didn't lie to him. Everything I did, felt, and said was the truth, even if it was the twisted truth.

"I wouldn't risk getting blood on my favorite pair of boots," I say.

He tosses the ball in the air again, ignoring me.

"But I'm done being nice."

Catch, toss, catch, toss...

I bite my lip to keep my frustration in. Spitting harsh words at him has no effect. The pain I inflict has to be physical. Hurting Zeke, spilling his blood, and scarring his body won't get him to talk, but at least I can tell Julian I tried everything.

But the thought of scarring Zeke's beautiful skin, cutting through his tattoos, and penetrating his muscles makes me sick. It will be more torturous for me than him.

I need something quick and effective. Something that will inflict the most pain with the least amount of effort. I've tortured plenty of men before. It's basically my job. But with Zeke—something stops me. Maybe it's knowing he didn't sell all those women—he saved them—that keeps me from wanting to hurt him.

Zeke studies me closely as he keeps tossing that stupid ball in the air. Whichever guard gave them the ball is going to get an ear chewing because it's driving me nuts right now.

"You don't have it in you to hurt me," Zeke says, smirking.

"Oh, really? Don't think I will hurt you? Tell me again how you ended up in that cage," I say.

Zeke stands up, tossing the ball on the bed—*thank god.* And then he walks over to the bars of his cage, his eyes never leaving mine.

"You may be an evil, selfish monster, but you don't enjoy torturing others. If you did, you would have done it by now.

You would have hurt me day one, not waited weeks, trying to butter me up to get me to talk. That's how I know you won't hurt me, at least not more than you already did. You played your hand too soon, sweetheart."

I snap.

I grab my gun from the waistband of my jeans. I aim. And fire.

Zeke howls at the impact of the bullet driving into his leg. I'm an excellent shot. Where I hit him will result in a high level of pain without risking him bleeding out too quickly. But from the grimace on Zeke's face, he was more concerned with the fact that the bullet was less than an inch away from hitting his most sensitive of areas.

"You were saying?" I say with a grin on my face. I lower my hand, letting the gun rest next to my leg. I have no intention of shooting Zeke again, but he doesn't know that.

He grabs the metal bars, and I'm not sure if the move is meant to intimidate me or if he's holding on to remain standing on his own two feet.

I see blood ooze out from his inner thigh and spill onto his dark jeans. Beads of sweat form on his forehead as his body heats and fills with adrenaline to deal with the pain. A natural response for the body to try to stop the spread of infection.

"Now, tell me something about your boss. Something we can use to track him down or penetrate his security systems. Just one tiny piece of information, and I'll get you some painkillers, antibiotics, and gauze to deal with that wound."

A half chuckle, half growl rumbles from his body. "You think shooting me in the leg, narrowly missing my crown jewels, hurts me enough to give up even the smallest information about my friends?"

"Nope. I think I could bring you to the edge of death, and you still wouldn't give them up."

"Then why did you shoot me?"

I shrug. "Because I'm tired of being underestimated. The reason I haven't tortured you isn't because I can't handle watching a man in pain. I've tortured plenty of men. I just know you. I know hurting you isn't the way to get you to tell me your secrets.

"That's why I didn't just capture and torture you like I would other men. It's why I didn't just pick you up in a bar and seduce you. You aren't that kind of man. Torture won't work."

I smile, looking at his wound. "But it does make me a little happy to know you won't question me again. Because next time, I won't aim for your leg. I'll see if hurting you in the most intimate of ways will get you to spill."

Zeke's jaw ticks.

I study his face turning white from loss of blood. He's so stubborn that he will literally pass out first before telling me anything. And I don't want to deal with having to call in a medical team to revive him.

But I can't let him know that.

I cross my arms, seeming bored. "Start talking before you pass out."

"I'm not going to pass out. I've been hit worse than this."

I nod. "I'm sure you have. But I doubt you've been hit in the groin like this. It shocks a man's system in a different way."

He shakes his head. "I've been hit worse, trust me."

I frown.

We both stare at each other, neither of us blinking. Whoever blinks first loses. It's the unspoken rule. If I blink, he knows I'll go get him something to take care of that wound. And if he blinks, I know he will spill in order to get the drugs.

We stare.

And dammit, he lets me into his soul. His soft eyes. His big heart. His selflessness. His need to protect, even in death, rather than ever hurt his friends.

I'm going to lose.

I blink.

He smirks triumphantly.

I scrunch my face in annoyance. "Sit your ass down while I go get you a Gatorade and some gauze to stop the bleeding. But if you think you are going to get a painkiller or a drop of alcohol without giving me information, you're crazy."

Zeke doesn't move, not until I've started climbing up the stairs. But as I reach the top, I hear the creak of the mattress as he sits down.

At least he won't pass out while I'm gone.

I return a few minutes later with the supplies: Gatorade, gauze, tweezers, thread, and a needle.

I toss Zeke the Gatorade, which he catches and chugs immediately without argument. He knows he needs to be hydrated so he won't pass out from the blood loss.

Then I slide the bag with the medical supplies to him. I probably shouldn't be giving him a needle, a potential weapon, but he needs it to close up the wound I caused. And having to do it without any numbing medication is another form of torture. I've stitched up myself enough times to know the sharp sting of a needle as it pierces flesh.

I slump down on the floor, feeling defeated.

"Thanks," Zeke says, holding up the bag before he digs through it to pull out the supplies.

God, he's such a gentleman even after I've been an ass to him.

What is wrong with him? I know men, and Zeke is so different than any man I've ever met before.

"Don't thank me."

"Sorry, I was taught manners. And I use them, even if you don't deserve them."

I shake my head, my hands falling between my legs. "This can't keep going on like this, Zeke. This has to end. You have to have a weak spot, some way to break you. Being nice, isn't it. Seducing you, isn't it. And torturing you, isn't it. What do I have to do to break you?"

"You had the right idea with the torture," Julian says, startling me as he speaks.

Zeke holds the gauze to his leg but stops rummaging through the bag.

I stand up, not liking being in such a vulnerable position around Julian.

Julian looks from me to Zeke. "You were just torturing the wrong person." Julian looks back at me.

"No," I say so softly that I'm not sure I even spoke the word.

Julian smirks, looking back at Zeke. "It worked before. You spilled your secrets just after I hurt her. Let's see if you still have feelings for her."

"He doesn't. He doesn't care about me that way anymore," I say, looking at Julian, pleading with my eyes for him to not hurt me again.

But I can see from his expression that he's not willing to stop without testing his theory. It worked before; he thinks it will work again. He hasn't spent time with Zeke these last few weeks, though. He doesn't know whatever connection we shared before has been broken. He doesn't know Zeke would rather watch me burn at the stake than ever say a word that could risk his friend's lives.

4

ZEKE

JULIAN WON'T HURT SIREN. She works for him. It would be stupid of him to hurt one of his best employees.

He did before, though.

No—whatever happened before wasn't real. It was a trick. A lie. He didn't hurt her.

But it sure felt real to me.

I close my eyes, remembering that night. I remember Siren lying naked and bound on the floor. Blood, gashes, and bruises covered her flawless skin. Her eyes were burning, and her legs were spread with Julian between them.

He didn't rape her. And he probably wouldn't have. He just wanted me to think he was going to.

But everything else was real. I felt the warm blood on her skin with my own hands. I saw the wounds on her flesh with my own eyes. I felt her heart slow in her chest. I watched her pass out from blood loss. I felt how weak she was in my arms. I smelt the alcohol he sprayed in her eyes and hoped that she would still be able to see afterward. I prayed next to her bed when her breathing got so weak I wasn't sure she'd wake up.

That was all real.

Julian really hurt her.

It wasn't fake.

He will hurt her again.

I open my eyes, the pain from that night igniting something inside me. I wince as I shift in place, and the bullet in my legs drills harder into my muscle. Siren hit me good in the leg. She's an excellent shot—to be that confident she would hit my leg and not my balls. *Or she didn't really care if she hit my balls.*

But she knew exactly where to shoot me to inflict the most pain. I don't think a single bullet has ever hurt me so much. My eyes are watering, begging me to let them cry. My teeth are grinding so hard together I'm sure I've broken at least one tooth. And my heart is jackhammering in my chest, trying to spread some pain relief throughout my body. But none of it is working.

I want some damn painkillers, alcohol, something to take this fucking hurt away. If I thought I could get away with lying to her about my boss in order to get the drugs, I would do it.

But the thought of watching Julian hurt Siren drowns out my whining thoughts about wanting painkillers.

Last time, I came into the room after he had already done the damage to her, but now, I'm going to have a front-row seat to the carnage.

Can I really just watch her get hurt without stepping in to save her?

I'm a protector. It's in my blood. *But what do I do when my choices are saving her or saving the only family I've ever known?*

Julian looks at me, and I show indifference. I press on my leg wound to distract me from what Julian is thinking of doing to Siren. *Thank god Julian can't read me as well as Siren can.*

When he turns his attention back to her, my eyes follow. And if I had any doubt about whether or not Julian would hurt her, the look on Siren's face erases it from my mind instantly.

Siren isn't a woman who is easily scared. In fact, the only time I've ever seen her truly petrified is around Julian.

But she's a fighter. She won't back down easily. She took me down even though she's less than half my size. Yes, I was distracted and not focused, but even if I wasn't, I wouldn't give myself the automatic win. She knows how to use her skills and body in ways I've never had to learn to do. I've always relied on my physical heft to get me through, while she uses her wit.

Last time Julian hurt her, she was tied up. The men who dragged her up there may have even held her down while Julian hurt her. Or she may have agreed to take the punches in order to do the job.

But the way Siren's eyes grow wide, the way her head shakes just a little, and the way she's already inching her hand toward her gun tells me that she didn't consent to Julian hurting her again. She isn't tied up or outnumbered like last time. This time, she will fight.

Good.

I won't have to make a decision. Siren can take care of herself. Yes, I may have to watch her take a punch or two, but that's the worst that will happen. If I just remain indifferent to Julian attacking her, she can hold her own until Julian gives up.

Julian takes a step toward her, and Siren takes a step back.

I frown.

That's not the woman I've come to know. She doesn't back down. But maybe she wants to keep her distance to draw out this tense situation and really sell her fear to me, hoping I'll give in.

Julian steps again; she retreats another step.

They continue like this, both dancing around each other.

I try to focus on the wound I should be dressing, but I can't take my eyes off of them.

I don't understand their relationship. He's her boss. And she clearly gives him her loyalty. *But why, if he hurts her? Even for a good reason?* Enzo Black would never hurt me. He'd never sacrifice my life or my pain to get something he wanted.

Julian slowly inches Siren back, until she's in the corner of the room. Her hands are by her side, ready to attack.

Grab your gun. Shoot the bastard!

But her hands don't move for the gun.

"Let's see how much you mean to the bastard," Julian says.

Punch.

It comes out of nowhere and lands square on her jaw.

I hear the crack.

I can feel it in my own jaw. I've taken enough punches to know exactly how it feels. And I say with certainty, it doesn't feel good. Your eyes immediately want to water, you taste the warm thickness of your own blood on your tongue, and you see stars for a split second.

That's what Siren is going through.

Stop being Aria and turn back into Siren—the woman who calculates everything and would only take a punch if she knew she could deliver something better in return.

I wait for her to fight back.

She doesn't.

I wait for her to reach for her gun.

She doesn't.

Instead, Siren stands strong in the corner of the room, a punching bag as Julian starts attacking.

Punch, kick, jab.

Each time he hits her, more blood spills.

She doesn't beg him to stop.

She doesn't attack.

She doesn't even throw up blocks to protect herself.

She just takes it, all of it.

Fight! Dammit, fight back!

Julian hits her exceptionally hard in the ribcage, and I know he bruised her ribs if not broke some.

That snaps her out of her spell.

This time he lunges, she blocks him, not willing to take anymore. And then she strikes back.

He dodges her hit, as her movements are slow now that she's lost considerable blood.

But she's fighting back. *Yes!* It will take her a second to gather her wits, to get her adrenaline pumping, and for the need to hurt him to push out her own pain. But once it does, she will fight back like a machine.

Instead, her eyes water with fear, and her lips seem to say I'm sorry.

What?

She shouldn't apologize to this monster. He hit her a dozen times.

Her eyes cut to me one last time. And I see everything— her fear, her pain, and her apology.

She won't fight back.

Her eyes break contact and return to her attacker.

Is this her last attempt to break me? To get me to save her over my friends? Or is there another reason she's not fighting back against Julian?

Whatever is happening, I don't understand. I just know that Siren is gone, and in her place is Aria. A beautiful, strong woman in her own right, but unlike Siren, Aria won't fight. She'll sacrifice herself to protect her boss, however misguided her thinking is. She's a lot like me in that way.

I prepared myself to watch her suffer. I can handle watching her in pain. She's choosing this to try and break me. She's letting him hurt her to hurt me. *Don't let them win.*

"You surprise me, Zeke. I never thought you'd be one to enjoy watching a woman get hurt like this. But maybe I was wrong. Maybe you are the same kind of monster I am," Julian says.

He punches her in the face again, breaking her nose. I watch her cough up blood.

Fuck.

I can't sit here and do nothing much longer. *But what choice do I have?*

I feel my own eyes water, but I don't dare let them out. Julian can't see how much pain he's causing me. He has to be close to stopping.

He hits her again, and she stumbles. She's barely standing upright.

This is almost over. *Just hold on for a few more seconds.* But I don't know if I'm telling her that or myself.

Julian's eyes light up watching Siren stumble.

I'm going to kill him. He deserves to die for this moment alone.

Julian looks back to me as Siren falls to her knees, silently pleading for this to be over. She wants him to knock her out so she won't have to feel, or even remember, this pain.

I don't know if I want him to knock her unconscious or not. I just can't watch her in pain anymore.

This next one is the final strike. I know it.

Julian stares at my wound, and then he pulls something from his pocket—a syringe.

"Here," he tosses the needle to me. "For the pain in your leg."

I catch the syringe staring at it cautiously. *Why is he easing my physical pain?*

Julian reaches back and pulls something else out —a gun.

"No!" I scream, but I'm too late.

He shoots her in the leg, in the same spot she shot me.

The syringe falls from my hands onto my crumple of blankets and pillows as I watch Siren writhe on the floor in pain. But unfortunately or fortunately, she doesn't pass out.

"Well—well, I guess I was right. You do have a conscious," Julian says, smiling.

I grab the bars, looking down at Siren covered in blood and pain. She doesn't look at me. She just lies still. She doesn't even grip her gunshot leg.

"Tell me something that can help me locate Mr. Black, or I'll shoot her again. And this time, I won't be so kind with my bullet placement," Julian says.

I stare down at Siren. *Hold on. I'll save you, just hold on.*

"Enzo Black has family in Greece. That is why he was there. Locate his family there, and you'll be able to set a trap for the next time he heads to Greece," I say.

Julian grins. "That wasn't so hard, was it?"

I ignore him and stare at Siren, who still isn't moving or speaking.

Julian looks down at her. "Get yourself cleaned up, and meet me in my office by six. We have work to do."

And then Julian leaves, not bothering to help Siren at all.

I watch her carefully, hoping she won't pass out now because there is nothing I can do to help her if she does. Her eyes close tightly as a single tear rolls down her cheek.

"Why do you work for him?" I ask.

She doesn't answer.

"Why didn't you fight back?" I ask.

No answer.

I sigh.

And then I hobble back to the medical bag and syringe on the floor. One plunge of the needle into my leg would give me incredible relief. But there is only one syringe, and Siren needs it more than I do.

"Here," I say, holding out the medicine.

Siren looks at me finally, her eyes wide as she stares at what I'm offering her—relief from her pain, while I get none.

She shakes her head. "You really don't understand that you need to stop saving me, do you?"

"Saving people is what I do, even undeserving people."

Slowly, she sits up, and I realize Julian's aim isn't as good as hers. He hit an artery. She's going to bleed out within minutes.

"Get the hell over here so I can stitch you up before you bleed to death," I say.

She glances down and then inches over as I crumple onto the ground.

"Hand me the gauze," she says.

I do, and she holds it on her leg to stop the bleeding. She leans against the bars; her breathing slow and weak. She's barely staying awake. But when her eyes look up at me, I know she has something she wants to say.

"Let's hear it," I say.

"Julian will realize you lied. You won't be able to get away with doing that a second time. But..." she moans. "But thank you for saving my life. He wouldn't have stopped until he killed me. So thank you, even though I don't deserve it. Even though, in the end, you'd be better off if I were dead."

She's killing me with her gratitude.

And I can't stand to see her in pain anymore.

So in a moment of weakness, I do what will ultimately stop my own pain. I grab the syringe and plunge it into her leg.

I do what I always do—I save her instead of myself.

5

SIREN

"YOU SHOULDN'T HAVE DONE THAT," I say, staring down at where Zeke plunged the needle into my leg.

The warmth of the drugs immediately starts spreading, sending new signals of comfort through my nerves—instead of pain.

I take a deep breath in and out. The stabbing, sharp pain leaves my leg and is replaced with a dull ache, matching the rest of my body.

I need to have a word with Julian. It's not okay for him to beat me every time he wants to get Zeke to talk. I'll be dead by the end of the week if he keeps this up.

"Yes, I should have," Zeke's husky voice brings me back to reality. I'll figure out how to deal with Julian later. Right now, I have a bullet in my leg, broken ribs, and a shattered nose. It hurts to breathe, and I don't even want to think about the pain of standing, even with the narcotics soothing me.

I look up at Zeke and see him painfully staring down at me. But not pain from his own wounds. He's not even gripping his leg anymore. He's looking at me in agony. His eyes

35

run over every injury on my body, assessing the damage, trying to pull my pain from my body with his eyes.

I'm still his weakness. He'd rather be in pain than watch me struggle. Julian was right. Even after everything I've done to Zeke, he's still willing to protect me. And it will be his downfall.

"Here," Zeke says, pushing the medic bag through the slits of the bars. He was shot in the same spot I was, but again, he puts my needs above his own. Yes, he doesn't have any other physical injuries, like I do, but we share the most serious wound. And he needs treatment as much as I do.

I push the bag back through the gap.

"You need this," Zeke says, trying to push it back through.

"Stop." I give him a stern look.

He moves to fight me again, but I wince as the bag hits my leg, and he stops. My moan is much louder than necessary to get my point across, but I need him to listen to me.

I scoot my body around to face the door of Zeke's cage. I can feel his gaze on me, but I don't turn to look or stop to explain to him what I'm doing.

Reaching the door is the easy part; the hard part comes next.

I grab one of the bars and start lifting my body up.

"Siren, stop!" Zeke says, running to the door in an instant like he isn't injured at all. He calls me by Siren instead of Aria, like he forgot my real name. And I don't know which name I prefer falling from his lips. *Any name, as long as it isn't 'lying bitch.'*

"No, it's my turn to protect you."

He frowns.

I pull myself up, standing on my good leg as I reach into

my back pocket and pull out the key that opens Zeke's cell. A key I haven't used since I first locked him in this cage.

I push the key in the lock and turn; the spring of the lock immediately clicking. I push on the bar door, and it falls open.

I lose my balance as I'm only standing on one leg, and I was leaning too harshly against the bar door.

I'm going to fall to the ground, and it's going to hurt. I don't even have the strength to catch my fall with my outstretched hands.

But instead of hitting the ground, I hit something else. Something equally as strong, but also soft—Zeke. His arms absorb most of my fall, but my head collides with his chest.

A shock of electricity surges through my body at the contact. I feel alive again. The pain shatters. And I want...I want more of this. I just want to be held in his arms, where I feel safe.

"Easy," Zeke says, as he slowly lowers us to the ground. His hands never leave my body.

My head continues to rest against his chest as I sit between his legs.

"We need to fix this," Zeke says, running his hand over my thigh near my wound.

I lean back against his chest and turn so I can see his wound, and then I do the same, my hand feeling his thigh muscles flex. "And this."

Zeke reaches around me to grab the medical bag. He digs in and pulls out a pair of tweezers and rubbing alcohol.

"Don't look," he says.

I bite my lip, smiling. "You numbed my leg, remember? I won't be able to feel anything."

"That's not what I'm worried about."

I tilt my head up and see Zeke look into my eyes. He's

afraid I will groan anyway. That I will have pain in my eyes. That it will hurt him too much to cause me any pain.

It's sweet—Zeke is sweet. But I don't like sweet.

I roll my eyes and grab the tweezers from his hand. Then I dig into my wound and pull out the bullet before tossing it on the ground outside of the cage. Then I press a piece of gauze over my leg.

Zeke shakes his head in awe. "You're something else, Siren."

"Aria."

"No, when you are being a badass, you're Siren."

I frown. "Aria is pretty badass too."

Zeke strokes my face. "No, Aria is courageous and sweet. Siren kicks ass."

I smile and then look down at his wound. "Do you want me to do the honors? Or would you like to do it?"

Even though pulling the bullet from my own leg was uncomfortable, it's nothing compared to what Zeke will feel with a pair of tweezers in his leg. He's not numb. I was.

"You do it," he surprises me by saying.

"I wish I had some alcohol or something to offer you for the pain."

He chuckles. "This is nothing, remember? You have no idea what my past life was like. I got shot on a weekly basis."

He places his hand on mine, where I'm holding the blood-soaked gauze to my own wound. I slip my hand out from beneath his, and then he applies pressure, the blood instantly slowing again.

I hold the tweezers in my other hand and then move to examine his would. The bullet looks deep, not near the surface. I use my left hand to gently open the wound so I can get a better look. And then I dive in, knowing the faster I get this done, the faster his pain will stop.

It takes me about ten seconds to find the bullet and pull it out. As I do, one of his arteries starts squirting blood.

Shit.

I grab gauze and apply hard pressure.

Stop, please stop.

Zeke doesn't move. He doesn't moan. He doesn't even flinch at the pain he must be drowning in.

"I need the needle and thread, now," I say calmly, not letting up my pressure.

Zeke doesn't move fast enough. At this rate, he'll bleed to death.

I grab for the bag and find the items I need. But I need Zeke to apply hard pressure while I start stitching.

"Give me your hands," I say.

"But—"

"Now," I snap, not caring about my own wound right now. He needs to apply a lot of pressure or he'll bleed out and die before I can get upstairs to call an ambulance.

I grab Zeke's hands and put them on his leg. I pull off my shirt and tie it around his thigh, making a tourniquet.

Zeke starts moving his hands.

"Don't you dare move. You move, you die."

He stills, immediately.

I start pushing the needle through his flesh, not caring how gentle I'm being or that he doesn't have any painkillers to numb his agony. I work quickly and efficiently, mending the artery and closing up the wound in his leg. Every second that passes feels like an hour.

Finally, I finish. Zeke removes my shirt from around his leg, and he carefully moves his hands away.

I look up at him. He looks pale, but he's still breathing. He's going to make it.

"My turn," he says, lifting my leg up onto his lap.

I don't argue with him.

He finds a new needle and thread and goes to work on my wound. His fingers are slow and gentle, unlike my furious stitch job. My bleeding isn't as bad as his, and my pain is numbed, so I can barely feel a thing. But for a moment, I wish that I could feel, even the pain. Because then it would be easier to feel the brush of Zeke's fingers against my skin.

Finally, he finishes the last loop.

And then we are left staring at each other. I'm in nothing but my bra and jeans. I'm still bloodied and bruised, but I can barely feel anything other than my need to say so much, and yet not being able to say anything, to Zeke.

And from the look on Zeke's face, he wants to speak to me too.

But neither of us say a word.

Zeke digs through the bag and finds a fresh cloth. Then he grabs my chin gently and begins wiping my face with it. It's only then that I realize how much blood and sweat are covering my body. He starts with my face, neck, then shoulders. His hand trails over my breasts and then eases over my badly bruised ribs. He stops when he gets to my blood-caked jeans.

His eyes look up at mine, asking for permission.

I nod.

His coarse fingers unbutton my jeans, then unzip the zipper, and finally, he begins pushing the jeans off my hips. It's not meant to be sexual. He moves more like a caretaker undressing me. But the heat from his fingers, the lust in his eyes, and his teeth biting his lip tell me that this could turn sexual in a moment.

Once my jeans are gone, he wipes the blood from my legs until I'm clean.

Then I turn and face him. He's just as bloody, even though his leg is the only damaged part of him. But I gaze at the hem of his shirt, wanting to do the same thing he did to me.

He nods, as I did.

And then I lift it, exposing his rippling muscles and tattoo-covered body. I dig out a clean cloth and begin cleaning his body of any remnants of blood. As I do, I notice things I didn't before—scars and healed bullet wounds. Someone did a number on his body. He's right in saying that the pain from one bullet is nothing compared to what he's used to handling.

I move to his jeans. I unbutton them, then unzip, ignoring the erection pressing against the zipper. And then I slowly start pulling the jeans down off his hips, trying to limit the pain I'm causing him. Eventually, his pants are free.

I clean away the blood on his legs, forcing myself to focus on his wound, his pain, and not on his enormous package I never got to explore. That might be my biggest regret: not letting him fuck me before I betrayed him. At least I would have that memory. Not that the memory of him licking me, bringing me to orgasm, is a bad memory— it's one of my favorites.

"Let me go see what alcohol or narcotics I can find for you," I say, moving to stand up.

But between my leg throbbing and Zeke grabbing my arm, I don't get far. I fall back against Zeke's warm chest and immediately close my eyes.

This—this is what I need.

Zeke drapes his arm around me, holding me to him.

"This is all I need—stay. The pain hurts less when you're here," Zeke says.

Zeke takes away my pain too.

I close my eyes and decide not to argue with him. It's probably not a smart move. The door to the cell is unlocked. Zeke could run if he wanted to. He could overpower me, hurt me.

But he won't.

Because unlike every other man in my life, Zeke is a good guy.

He saved me.

He protected all those women who Julian wanted him to sell.

And then he saved me again.

He put me first.

No other man has ever done that.

Slowly, I feel the pull of sleep overtake me. And I welcome it. Being in Zeke's arms will force me to dream of him. I'll dream of something I will never have.

Sleep pulls me under.

Sometime in the middle of the night, I wake. We are no longer sitting in the middle of the cell. We are lying on Zeke's bed. My head lies on his chest, and his arms are wrapped around me tightly. We are both practically naked, wearing only our underwear.

I shouldn't have stayed. I've stirred up feelings in both of us we can't act on.

But I feel safe in his arms, even though I shouldn't. Zeke could betray me as easily as I did him. Julian will encourage it. And I'll end up hurt again.

These feelings aren't real. It's just the drugs and pain talking.

I move to slip out from under Zeke's arm.

"Stay," Zeke says.

He doesn't open an eye, but I feel his arm constrict around me.

"Why? This won't end well. We shouldn't feel anything but hatred for each other."

He smiles with his eyes still closed. "I never was one for feeling what I should."

"What do you feel?"

He opens his eyes. "Safe."

I exhale a breath I didn't realize I was holding. *Safe*—I don't know what I was hoping he would feel, but safe wasn't the word I wanted. I wanted more, even though I don't deserve it. Although, what I should hope is that Zeke feels nothing, or better yet, feels hatred for me.

"Promise me, Zeke," I whisper against his neck so the cameras Julian placed won't be able to see.

"Promise what?"

"Promise me that when the time comes, you'll choose yourself."

He frowns.

"Don't choose to protect Mr. Black, or your friends, or your family, or me. Don't choose the innocent lives. Choose to save yourself."

It should be an easy promise. If he truly hates me, he'd make it easily.

Instead, he grunts, and then moments later, he's asleep as if it were all a dream. *Maybe it was.*

I should go.

But I don't, because I too feel safe.

So instead, I drift back to sleep in Zeke's arms and know that no matter what, I won't regret this moment tomorrow. Not for a second.

6

ZEKE

Choose you.

Her words haunt me all night. I dream about them, have nightmares about them. But every time I awoke and saw that Siren was still in my arms, I calmed.

I told her I felt safe with her here, and I do.

But I also feel so much more.

Lust.

Want.

Need.

My cock is fucking painful as it presses into her ass. I want her so badly. My one regret about how we spent our time together was never fucking her. I should have seduced her that first night. Then, we could have spent our entire time fucking instead of dancing around the issue.

Now it's too late.

My leg feels stiff and painful, but I won't move, not until she's awake. I'll cherish every moment of her in my arms. Because in my heart, I know this will be the last time. The last time I feel her warm skin against my bare chest. The last time I'll smell her sweet scent. The last time my heart will beat in sync with hers.

It will also be the last time I feel like this—like I want her. I want to kiss her.

The only reason I feel any of those things now is because Julian discovered my weakness. I can't stand to see others hurt—especially those who can't or won't fight back.

I don't know why Siren didn't fight back against Julian, but it killed me watching it happen. It stung every time I drove the needle through her body, closing her wound. And when she painfully whimpered out in her sleep, it was like my heart was being stabbed over and over.

Watching her suffer hurt me worse than getting shot.

But it doesn't change the fact that she betrayed me. She chose herself over me. And she will do it again.

I kiss her hair, taking a deep breath. Siren is beautiful and strong and incredible, but she's not mine. Her heart doesn't belong to me. She doesn't love me. I suspect she isn't even capable of love.

We have that in common. We will never love. But that is where we diverge. Because she will always choose herself, while I will always choose others.

I feel her stirring in my arms, and our time together is over. In the daylight, with our wounds closed, our hearts will shut too. But it was nice to imagine, even for a moment, that we could be something more.

Siren doesn't say anything as she slowly sits up, and this time, I let her. I don't pull her back into my empty arms.

She turns and looks at me, while I study her flawless skin. Yes, her skin is marked with scars, bruises, and injuries, but to me, it's flawless. Because it's her, and it represents how tough she is, like body armor.

I can tell she feels like she should put some clothes on,

but the only clothes for her to wear are covered in blood, sweat, and dirt on the floor.

I open my mouth to speak, but she puts a finger to my lips.

"I'll be right back," she says.

I frown, but let her go. It takes her a while to stand, her body adjusting to the pain in her leg, ribs, and face. The narcotics from last night have clearly worn off, but she doesn't make a sound or grimace as the pain consumes her body. She's focused and determined on her task.

Eventually, she starts walking. Magically, she makes it up the stairs. She doesn't bother locking the door. *I could make a run for it.*

But I don't. I want her to come back. And I can't leave until I have a plan to kill Julian.

A few minutes later, she returns with a bottle of whiskey and clothes in her hands.

She stumbles, and I jump up intending to catch her, but my leg gives out, and I fall back into the bed. Apparently, taking it slow like Siren did is the way to go.

She recovers from her stumble and shakes her head. "You will never put yourself first, will you?"

She holds out the whiskey bottle to me. I take it and take a swift drink. Alcohol isn't always the best for healing, but it sure helps with the pain. And I'm tired of acting like my own suffering means nothing.

I hold it back to her, but she shakes her head.

"Siren," I say sternly.

She takes the whiskey bottle and takes a long drink.

I smile.

But then she holds out clothes, and I frown.

She laughs.

"Get dressed, I'm tired of looking at your scrawny, ugly ass body," she teases.

"Ugly? And scrawny? Huh?"

She nods playfully.

I snatch all the clothes from her hands. "Fine, but I'll need all of these clothes to cover my body then. I wouldn't want you to have to look at an inch of my ugly ass."

She tries to grab back one of the T-shirts she intended to wear. But I hold it high out of reach. But then she jumps, and the impact of her hitting the ground again brings us both back to reality.

"Fuck, Siren!"

I grab her and pull her back into my arms as I study her leg.

"You popped a stitch," I say.

She looks down at the trail of blood trickling down her inner thigh. I wipe the blood away with my thumb, and then I suck it.

Her eyes grow big, and she bites her bottom lip. "I'm not sure if that was the sexiest thing I've ever seen, or the grossest."

I laugh. "Let me fix you up."

I pull her into my lap, and then she leans back to grab the medical kit. I pull out the items I need and then get to work stitching her up. I'm very aware she doesn't have any narcotics numbing her skin his time. So I hesitate.

"Just stab me already. Take out your anger on my skin," she says with a smile.

I roll my eyes and then do as she says.

She moans dramatically, like I've just shot her again.

I stop. *Did I really hurt her?*

She laughs. "God, you're gullible. If I was a better actress, I could get you to do anything I wanted."

"I thought you didn't lie?"

"I don't."

"What was that, then?"

"Acting, and very bad acting at that."

I want to ask her the next question—*why can't she lie?*

But I don't. I have a million questions, but none of them I ask.

I push the needle through her skin again, carefully this time, but she doesn't move or moan or make any sound to indicate that I hurt her. I've stitched up buddies before, but never a woman. And never my enemy.

She's my enemy—I have to remember that.

I finish the stitch, and then I look up. Siren is staring into my eyes with such emotion that I can't read her expression.

She's two women—Aria and Siren. My enemy and a woman I could love with everything I have.

My hand strokes her thigh automatically; her skin warms under my touch. Her skin isn't the only thing that warms—her eyes soften and her lips part.

I want her.

She wants me.

She's still not wearing a shirt or pants, and I'm dying to explore all of her body—her breasts, her stomach, and I need to get reacquainted with her pussy. The way she's staring at my chest, abs, and biceps; the way she avoids looking down to see my growing erection, all tell me she wants to get to know my body too, even though she won't admit it.

I lean close, so close that a heavy breath could push our lips together. So close that kissing her seems inevitable instead of just something I want.

My siren doesn't move away. But she doesn't close the gap. I won't close the gap either. I won't make the first move, not after what she did to me. But I won't stop this from happening either.

I *need* this to happen. I need to finish the physical connection we started—fuck Siren out of my system. Use her and then hurt her like she did me. Have my one moment with Siren and then turn her into Aria, the sweet girl I want nothing to do with.

The moment stretches into infinity. Both of us too stubborn to move the final inch, both too needy to move away.

My gaze falls down to her bra. *Maybe it will just snap open?* The straps look pretty thin and worn after all.

Jesus, I can't keep this up much longer. I need to move. I need to taste her.

Her breath heats against my mouth. *Yes, just give in, Siren.*

She closes her eyes. She's going to falter. She's going to kiss me.

"Truth or sin?" she says, her eyes opening in pain.

"What?" I ask, shocked that she spoke instead of kissing me.

She stands up and grabs the clothes I dropped on the floor next to us. She grabs an oversized shirt and slips it over her body, wearing it like a dress. Then she picks up another shirt and sweatpants and hands them to me.

The moment has passed, so I don't argue, taking the clothes from her and putting them on. With us dressed, our hormones won't get the best of us again. I will never kiss Siren again. I may never even have an excuse to touch her skin.

I nod. She wants to play this game, so she goes first.

Siren sits down, crossing her legs in front of her like a child, instead of the serpent she is. I wait for her question. A question I won't answer—about my former boss, about my friends. *Not going to happen.* But it means she will get to commit a sin if I don't answer her question with the truth.

Her eyes read my thoughts, and she smiles—such a beautiful genuine smile.

Don't fall for it.

"Why did you plunge that syringe into my leg instead of your own?" she asks.

I frown. She gave me an easy question she already knows the answer to. *Does she think me answering is going to make me feel weak?* Because being who I am will never make me feel anything but strong.

My eyes sear into hers, as I shift my weight forward and sit on the edge of the mattress on the floor, leaning as close to her as possible. "You already know my answer, but since you don't trust actions, only words—the truth is I couldn't handle seeing you in pain. Watching you thrash in pain was worse than my own pain. To stop my own torment, I had to stop yours. You are still my weakness," I say, admitting everything. It's the truth, and she knows it. It's why I told Julian a lie to protect her. She may think she's the only special one, but she isn't. I save and protect people. Put any other woman in Siren's place, and I would have done the same thing.

"But don't think for a second that just because I don't like seeing you suffer, it means that I will always protect you. That ship sailed the second you sold me out to Julian."

Her smile brightens. "Good, because I don't want you to save me, Zeke. I never have."

I growl and attack her without thinking. She's on her back, and I'm sprawled on top of her. My leg spreads hers, my breath coats her face, and my arms have her pinned beneath me.

She's not scared though, nor pissed. In fact, she's turned

on seeing this side of me, the side that takes instead of asking.

Her eyes light up, looking at me. "Your turn."

Dammit, this is probably part of her game. Get me so turned on I can't think straight to get me to ask an easy, softball question instead of one where I get to sin. I take a deep breath, trying to clear Siren from my thoughts. *Like that's going to happen.* I need to fuck her, then I can get her out of my head, and my cock can stop begging for her. It will realize she's just like any other woman I've ever fucked. My brain will realize that even though she has boobs and a pussy, she is basically an extension of Julian—my enemy, a person I need to take out, not protect.

I open my mouth to speak but stop. I debate which question I want the answer to before finally deciding. "Why didn't you fight back against Julian?"

She doesn't break eye contact, not even to bat her eyelashes at me.

"Sin."

She arches her back, her pointed nipples poking through her bra and T-shirt and stabbing me in the chest. I push my groin higher up against her soaked panties. Her eyes darken, and she licks her luscious lips—lips I haven't tasted in far too long.

"Screw it," I say and do both what I want and shouldn't do, which makes this a sin—I kiss her.

Our lips crash together in a sexy ambush. She can't move beneath me, and I grip her wrists to keep myself from exploring too much of her body too quickly. I just focus on her lips. Her fucking swollen lips know exactly how to kiss me. Her lips part just enough to allow plenty of tongue, and what a magnificent tongue she has. It has so many more talents than just lying to me and pretending to only speak the truth. Her tongue teases and taunts mine, before finally surrendering.

But God, her moans are intoxicating. I could live off her sweet moans. They penetrate every ounce of my body and shoot straight to my cock. I'm desperate for her. My cock is throbbing between her legs, and I could easily rip the clothes that separate us and drive through until I'm buried deep inside her.

She tries to move her wrists, desperate to tangle her hands in my hair as much as I am to tangle my hands in hers. We both want this sin with everything we have.

We want this kiss to never end.

We want this kiss to turn to more.

We want this kiss to become fucking.

I slowly let go of her wrist, needing to feel more of her soft flesh, but not wanting her to have too much power. I don't even want to give her the ability to control her own hand, but needing to feel her skin wins out.

I run my hand up her thigh as I continue to taste her mouth. Slowing my kisses as I feel more of her, taking my time, so I get to experience all of her.

My hand slides up her side, pushing the T-shirt she is wearing up her smooth skin.

"I wish I could enjoy my sin without you enjoying it as well." I bite her lip, sucking it furiously, and I instantly feel her soak my sweatpants between her legs. "But I know that you are going to enjoy this sin as much as I will."

The sound of footsteps startles me. I instantly jerk Siren up and into my arms and away from whatever danger is approaching. But from the slow, careful descent of the steps, I know who is approaching. And I don't know who he is more dangerous to—Siren or me.

Julian appears at the bottom of the stairs in a full suit,

like he's attending a formal dinner instead of creeping on us in the basement.

I look around the room searching for cameras, and I spot a dozen places where there are likely some hidden. That means he can see and hear every word Siren and I have said.

I shoot Siren a glare as I think back to everything we said or did. *What did Julian hear?* And he almost got to see what was mine—Siren, her body at least.

"Oh, don't stop on my account," Julian says, smiling.

"What do you want?" I ask.

"Just to say that your little tip was fake, a lie. It's something I wouldn't usually put up with, but after listening in on your little conversation, I got an idea."

I loosen my grip on Siren, who doesn't seem in any hurry to get out of my arms. It doesn't surprise me considering what Julian did to her, but he's still her boss, and I'm her enemy, why is she still in my arms?

"What is your brilliant idea? Releasing me and giving me a boat to leave on?"

Julian laughs. "I can see what the ladies see in you; you are a funny one." He walks further into the room, before leaning against the open door of the cell and crossing his arms as he looks from Siren to me.

"This truth or sin game seems intriguing. Have room for a third player?"

$$7$$

SIREN

I SHOULD HAVE BEEN MORE careful. I shouldn't have played our truth or sin game, knowing Julian had cameras hidden in the basement. I shouldn't have let Zeke kiss me...

But God, what a kiss.

Zeke's kisses are like nothing I've ever felt before. They are toe-curling, fireworks shooting, and every other cliché in the book. His kisses wreck my soul and make me wish I could kidnap Zeke and travel far away from here—start my life over with just him and me.

But that can never happen.

I've been careless, selfish even. I wanted Zeke to kiss me again. I wanted so much more than just a kiss. I wanted every physical thing Zeke was offering.

And I would have gotten it, if Julian hadn't interrupted. Some small part of me is thankful Julian did interrupt before I let things go too far. Because once I fuck Zeke, there is no going back. I can keep protecting my heart from falling for a man like Zeke, but my lady bits—that's another story.

I already know from the way Zeke kisses, from the way he licked me like I was his favorite flavor of ice cream, that if he fucked me, he would ruin me for any other man. No man would ever compare to him, and I would always crave Zeke. He would have the upper hand again, and I can't let that happen. I need to be in control. I need to manipulate him into giving up Enzo Black.

"The truth or sin game is invite-only, and I don't remember inviting you," Zeke answers, his voice deep and throaty.

Every word the man speaks is sexy and makes me constantly on edge and soaked with need.

Julian stares at me, like I'm his. *I guess I am.*

I'm usually comfortable wearing very little clothes. My body is fit and curvy, most men's dream body. And I flaunt it often. It's how I get information for Julian from men. But the only man in the world whose gaze scares me is Julian's.

I should have put pants on. And a baggy sweatshirt. Anything to cover every inch of my skin, because the way Julian is looking at me scares the hell out of me. I can't tell if he wants to taste me, fuck me, or beat me.

Julian laughs. "I think you are forgetting one important detail. You don't get a say in your life anymore. You are locked in that cell, and I'm out here, so I suggest you hear my proposal."

Zeke raises an eyebrow as he runs his hand up my ass and over my smooth stomach like he owns me. I love the feeling of his hand on my skin. I love him taking charge over my body, demanding me to surrender to him. But I don't like him doing it with Julian in the room.

Zeke nods to the cell door. "Seems I've already figured out how to get the door open. I don't think I'm the one whose trapped or should be worried. I would sleep with one eye open if I were you."

"Cockiness doesn't suit you, Zeke." Julian looks at me and snaps his fingers.

I hate being called like a dog, but I'd rather not get beaten or shot again. So I comply. I reluctantly climb out from under Zeke. The ache in my heart is worse than the ache in my leg as I stand, and Zeke's hands fall from my body. He is no longer willing to protect me, not when I'm following Julian's orders. And I don't blame him.

It's better this way.

Knowing it's right doesn't temper the pain from walking away from Zeke, again. And from knowing that this time might be really goodbye. This time will put us squarely on different sides of the line. Enemy versus enemy. There will be no going back. We won't be able to protect each other anymore. I have to protect myself, and Zeke is insistent on protecting Enzo Black and his family.

I pull the T-shirt I'm wearing down until it's covering my ass again, and then I walk proudly over to Julian, like I'd prefer to be by his side instead of Zeke's.

Julian strokes my hair in the way I wish Zeke had the chance to do.

"You are just as trapped as ever, Zeke. You just fell for Aria's beauty and spell again," Julian says.

Zeke doesn't look at me. He doesn't change his expression at all, like the comment didn't even hurt him. Like I mean nothing to him. Not like he didn't just have me trapped and writhing under his body, as his erection pushed between my legs. He can pretend all he wants that I mean nothing to him, but I know the truth. His body can't lie to me.

Julian smirks. "Now, as I was saying. I would like to make you an offer."

"There is nothing you can say to make me turn on my friends," Zeke says.

Julian plays with the ends of my hair as he looks from me to Zeke. His eyes eventually land on the wound Zeke stitched up, more evidence of Zeke's lust for me.

"I'm sure I can find some reason that you might reconsider giving up your friends for," Julian says, referring to me. He doesn't realize Zeke only wants me for my body. He doesn't care about me. He doesn't love me. He doesn't even like me.

"Never," Zeke says.

Julian lets go of my hair, and my stomach settles just a little.

"I thought you'd say that, which is why my deal includes an option other than spilling your friends' secrets," Julian says.

Zeke narrows his gaze, his teeth snarling like a wolf about to attack.

I stand still, watching the two men threaten each other with their bodies.

"As I said before, I'd like to play the truth or sin game with you," Julian says.

Zeke turns up his nose and makes a disgusted look. "You do understand that when I say truth or sin, that sin means something sexual. You may be into men, but I have no desire to fuck you, Julian."

"I think you'd very much like to fuck me, and that's why you'll say yes to my arrangement."

Zeke doesn't spit a comeback. He just waits to hear what sneaky deal Julian has come up with that will more than likely be a win-win for Julian and a lose-lose for Zeke.

"I don't care how you play the game with Aria. With me, the rules are simple. We will play five rounds. Well—you will play five rounds. I won't be offering up any truths or sins of my own," Julian says.

There it is. Julian will play the game by not having to risk anything in the first place.

"Each round, I will offer you a chance to answer a simple question with the truth. If you refuse, you will complete a sin. Any sin that I choose."

"And what's in it for me?" Zeke asks.

Nothing, nothing is in it for you. The sooner you figure that out, Zeke, the sooner you will figure out how to get free.

"Once you complete all five rounds, I'll set you free. I'll even throw in a boat."

"That's not good enough," Zeke answers.

"I figured it wouldn't be." Julian cuts his eyes to me and winks, like he and I are in cahoots. The truth is, I'm on nobody's side but my own. "I also promise not to harm Mr. Black until you have completed all five rounds."

Zeke's pupils dilate. *Julian's got him.* Zeke could protect his boss for as long as the five rounds go on, and as soon as the game is over, he could run to his friends' rescue. All Zeke ever wants is to protect those he loves. I don't know exactly how many people that includes, but I know it's Mr. Black and the immediate people around him. Zeke will take the deal.

I try to catch Zeke's attention, to warn him with my eyes, my tight lips, my clenched jaw. But he doesn't glance my way. And even if he did, I doubt he would listen to me.

Julian, on the other hand, is practically giddy. He knows that Zeke will accept his offer. He knows Zeke's weakness.

"I'll throw in one more sweetener," Julian says.

I still—I don't like the sound of that. Julian never offers something for nothing.

Zeke practically growls in response. He, too, knows that

Julian isn't going to offer something without asking for more in return.

Julian wraps his arm around my waist and pulls me tightly to his side, stroking my hip over my shirt. If he so much as slips his hand beneath my shirt, I'm going to kill him. I put my hand on top of Julian's, not even pretending to enjoy his touch. I dig my nails into his hand so hard that I'm sure I'm making him bleed.

Julian, to his credit, doesn't wince, hiss, or pull his hand away. He just takes the pain like he deserves it.

Zeke's lip curls up the tiniest bit, and I know he sees my nails digging into Julian's hand.

"To give you a little more incentive to complete the sins or tell the truth, you'll be playing with Aria's life," Julian says.

I frown, my hand pushing Julian's off my body as I stare at him incredulously. He can't bargain with my life. He has no right. I'm his employee. His best employee, in fact. He can't just decide that he can offer up my life if Zeke fails.

"You complete the five rounds by either telling the truth or completing the sins, and Aria lives. If you lie, or fail to complete a single one of the sins, then Aria dies," Julian says.

I narrow my gaze and tighten my lips. I can't call out Julian's bluff for what it is—a lie. Julian would never kill me. But the bullet in my leg would feel like a scratch if I outed Julian to Zeke.

"And if I decline your offer entirely?" Zeke asks.

Julian grins, thinking he's won. He knows exactly how to take out Zeke.

"Then I'll kill Aria and go after Mr. Black on my own."

I swallow hard.

Lies.

They're all lies!

Don't make the deal, Zeke. It will destroy you.

But some tiny part of me wants Zeke to agree. I want to know that he is still willing to put my life before his own. I still want to be under Zeke's protection. I want him to save me, even at the expense of himself.

Now, it's Zeke's turn to laugh. "Really? That's your offer? Take your deal, or you'll kill Aria?" Zeke's beautiful eyes look to me, taunting me with his disgust for me. "I've wanted Aria dead since the moment I learned she was working for you. So the fact that you'll do it for me if I refuse just incentivizes me to turn down your offer."

"So is that your decision? You are refusing my offer?" Julian asks, with a smile.

Fuck, this is all part of Julian's plan. There is no way for Zeke to win.

"Yes, I decline your offer. I'd rather stay in this cell for the rest of my life than take your deal."

Julian chuckles and then links his arm through mine. "Well, that answers that question. I guess he doesn't love you, after all, Aria. He doesn't care if you live or die, which means you are of no more use to me. Tomorrow, you die."

My eyes cut to Zeke. I know that Julian is bluffing, but Zeke doesn't. I study Zeke's reaction; his face is unmoved. His eyes don't widen with worry; his lips don't tense with fret; his heart doesn't thump wildly begging Julian to reconsider.

Zeke truly doesn't care if I live or die.

Even though I know Julian won't kill me tomorrow, it still hurts knowing that Zeke will no longer protect me.

8

ZEKE

I SHOULD HAVE SAID YES. I should have accepted Julian's offer, but I couldn't let Siren have the upper hand again. I couldn't let her know that I care about her, even the tiniest bit. She can't have control over me, not again.

I stare at the floor as Siren walks to the cell door, closes it, and then locks it. I can feel her eyes on me, even though I refuse to return her gaze. But I hear the clink of the door and the clank of the lock as the door closes, and I feel her stare on me.

She takes a heavy breath, sighing before following Julian up the stairs.

And then I'm alone. Except for the security cameras, I'm truly alone for the first time in weeks. No guard. No Julian. And no Siren.

Just me with my thoughts and regret.

I made my decision to save myself instead of Siren, but only because I don't truly think she is in any danger. Julian won't kill her. He'll hurt her, torture her, but not kill her. She's too valuable to him.

But what if I'm wrong?

What if he kills her?

What if I chose myself over her?

I shake the thought from my head. I have more important things to worry about right now—like how to get out of here and protect my friends from Julian.

I walk back to the bed and sit down; my leg is sore and achy. But then I spot the bottle of whiskey Siren brought in. She didn't take it with her. I grab the bottle and take a long swig, quickly feeling the sting of pain reducing.

At least I have this bottle to keep me comfortable.

I move my legs to swing them onto the mattress, but my leg bumps into something. I look down—the medical bag. Siren left it.

I grab the bag and quickly rummage through it to find something to use to unlock the door. I keep my ears open, listening carefully in case a guard comes downstairs, so I can hide the bag quickly if one does. This bag holds the key to my escape; I can't let anyone know I have it.

I find a needle.

And then look to the door. *Should I try it now or wait?*

I can't wait. There aren't any guards watching me, at least none in the basement. This might be my only chance. Even if a guard is watching me on the security cameras, it could take a minute or two for them to get down here. This is my only chance.

I run to the door, quickly loop my arms through the bars, and press the needle inside the lock.

One...

Two...

Three...I feel the rattle of the lock turning over, and then I gently push the door open.

I'm free of my cage.

Now, I need to save my friends. I need to escape. But most of all, I need to kill Julian.

I creep carefully up the stairs, completely silent, so if a guard is waiting upstairs, they won't hear me.

I open the door to the main floor of the house I stayed in for months. A house that was just as much a cage as the bars holding me in the basement, even though it might have been a bit more comfortable.

I squint as the sunlight hits my eyes for the first time in months. I blink several times, trying to adjust. And right now, I can't decide if I missed the sun or want it to go away again.

Finally refocused, I look around my house and find no guards.

My heart lightens with hope. I might really be able to get free. Or at the very least, protect my friends by killing Julian.

But if I fail, I at least need to warn them.

I move through the shadows of the house until I find one of the guns I hid in the floorboard of the pantry. I pull it out and put it in the back of my pants. Outside the pantry, I find paper, an envelope, and a pen. I stick them all in my pocket.

My time is running out to stay undetected in this house. I need to leave and hide until darkness falls, then I can carry out the second part of my plan.

So that's exactly what I do. I run outside and down the beach, away from Julian's property, until I reach a neighbor's backyard filled with enough bushes and trees for me to hide in until nightfall.

If I only wanted to save myself, then I should be in search of a boat. But as usual, I'm at the bottom of my own priority list. I need to save my friends, and the only way to do that is to kill Julian and...Siren, if I have the strength to do it.

Siren may follow orders now, but if I kill Julian, she will be the one in charge. He may not have announced her as her second, but since he put her on the most important task he had—*me*, I know that she would take over. And she would continue her boss's mission.

I can't let that happen.

I shouldn't distract myself with thinking about Siren. Right now, I need to warn my friends, and I need to kill Julian.

I take out the pen and paper to write to them in warning. I put my pen to the paper to write to Enzo, but at the last second change my mind, and instead write to Kai.

I smile as I think about Kai's future. About how strong she is and how she will one day rule—either by Enzo's side or on her own. She will claim the Black kingdom; I have no doubt.

Thinking of Kai reminds me of who Siren really is—how strong she is. I can't leave Siren alone. Because she will claim her power, the same as Kai.

———

Darkness falls hours later. My feet have fallen asleep, my leg has swollen, and my back aches from leaning against a palm tree and squatting behind a bush all afternoon.

I'm thirsty, hungry, and exhausted.

But I'm more determined than ever.

I move through the night, silent as the gentle wind, barely making a whisper for anyone to discover me.

I know enough about Julian Reed's property and routine to know I'll be faced with a high tech security system and dozens of guards when I reach his property. But nothing and no one is going to stop me from completing my mission.

I move across the property, crouching below windows, as I make my way to Julian's house. I need to get into the garage, that's where the power is. I won't be able to disable the security system junction box, since he has it locked up in a vault, but I can disable the power, which should shut off the security system for a few minutes.

I pop the garage side door open, find the power, and disable it. The hiss of the electricity immediately dies. Then I hear the shuffle of men inside. I draw my gun, careful to know exactly how many bullets I have left—six—and that I need to preserve at least one for Julian.

I wait in the shadows as the men throw the house door open and start flowing into the garage.

Pop.

Pop.

Pop.

I take out the three men that ran inside the garage. I run to the first man and take his gun, then quickly make my way over the dead bodies and up the stairs into the house.

The house is silent, but that doesn't shock me. The first men attacked loudly and wildly, but the rest of the men will hide and wait to attack me unannounced.

Behind each corner and each wall is a possible threat. But I take my time. I have all fucking night. And this is where I thrive. Even with a bum leg, I love the adrenaline of hunting men down and making them suffer.

I hear the creak of a floorboard in the silence.

Mistake number one.

I turn the corner and fire before the man even has a chance to aim his gun in my direction. I watch the man fall and hit the floor loudly. If the gunfire didn't already, it draws every man's attention to my location.

But I'm ready for them. Bring it on.

Fire.
Fire.
Fire.
And then...
Fall.
Fall.
Fall.

I take out every guard until I hear silence in the house. Not even the sound of another man breathing leaks into the tranquility. I've disabled the security system. I've taken out his guards. Now it's time to kill Julian Reed.

Even with my wounded leg, I run up the stairs of Julian's house. Ready to complete my mission. Ready for Julian to be dead.

I'm sure Julian has heard the commotion downstairs and is awake now, but when I get to his bedroom door, I hear snoring—loud and thunderous. I creak the door open enough for me to see him lying in the middle of his bed with a face mask and earplugs.

I grin.

He won't even see death coming.

Maybe I should torture him, but I'm not going to. I just want him dead. Torture won't protect my friends; only death will.

I push the door open. Then I aim my gun. I don't even need to go into his bedroom to kill him. I have excellent aim. I could have shot him from across the entire length of the property if all the buildings weren't blocking my way.

I begin to squeeze the trigger and then...

Bang.

My body slams into a wall, my hand barely gripping my gun as it smashes between my large frame and the drywall in the hallway. My head spins for a second from the abrupt impact, and I know that I just busted open the stitches holding my wound together.

But that's all I allow myself—one second of pain before I begin to attack back.

I spin, throwing the body off mine. Before I even look at my attacker, my instinct tells me who thwarted me.

Siren.

Still, my body automatically aims the gun in her direction. I can't pull the trigger, even if I should.

She smiles back at me. "Finally got the balls to aim that gun at me?"

I frown. "Still giving your loyalty to the wrong man?"

She glares, putting her hands up like she's about to enter a boxing match with me. "I'm loyal to no one but myself."

I raise an eyebrow, keeping the gun on her body. "You just saved your boss's life; I think you're loyal to him."

"You and your loyalty, Zeke. Sometimes people do things not out of loyalty but because they want to."

I cock my head to the side. "You and I don't." I don't know how I know her so well, but deep down, she's doing this out of loyalty. I just don't understand why she gives her loyalty to that monster.

Siren stares at the gun. "You going to shoot me? Or are we going to fight fair?"

"Fair? I don't think there is anything fair when it comes to us."

"You're right; we don't fight fair." And just like that, a knife flies at my hand and jabs into my palm, causing me to drop the gun.

I growl as blood pours out of the gash in my right hand.

And then we both run full speed toward each other—full of anger, frustration, lust, need. Everything fuses together. We both fuel it all into this one outburst of emotion about to collide.

And collide we do. Siren's legs wrap around my body as she tries to climb me like a spider. Her hands grip my hair and pull hard, her other fist plummeting into my neck.

In return, I slam her back hard against the wall, my arms dancing with hers, unable to decide if I'm trying to fling her off or pull her tighter.

Our bodies flush, full of blood and nerves, hopelessly in need of a release. But we aren't going to get it, at least not in the sexual way.

Siren digs her nails into my back, trying to get me to free her, but it's not going to happen.

"You're willing to fight me? Why don't you fight him?" I say into her hair, taking a deep breath of the flowery scent of her shampoo. The scent calms most of my body and hardens other parts.

Pain springs into my vision as she head-butts me, and we fall backward. I'm barely able to stay on my feet with Siren tangling her limbs around my body like she's trying to suffocate me.

"Is that the best you got?" I taunt her. "Because if so, this is going to be a quick fight."

She smirks. "Men and their cockiness. Just because I'm a woman, doesn't mean that I'm not capable of taking you down."

"You and what muscles?"

She laughs. "Fighting isn't about strength. Fighting is about knowing your enemy, knowing his weaknesses, and exploiting them."

"You may know my weakness, but there is nothing you can do to exploit it, when the people I care about aren't here."

She jumps back, "Maybe not, but the people you care about aren't your only weakness."

I feel like I've been stabbed as she presses her thumb into my wound. *Holy fucking hell!* That shouldn't hurt that bad, but it does.

I've never punched a woman. Never fought against one. Never had to hurt one. Maybe that's sexist to think that women are any less deserving of being fought than men are. But over the years, I've started to learn differently. Siren is the one who will finally correct my outdated thoughts.

Women are just as capable as men.

Siren lets go of me, and I grunt in pain, griping my leg like she just cut it off. She's walking toward the gun on the floor, and I have no doubt if she gets it, she'll shoot me. And I don't plan on getting shot again.

I run at her, letting go of the pain in my leg as I throw her over my shoulder. She yells, punching my back. "Put me down."

I slap her ass. "Not a chance."

I point the toe of my shoe under the gun, flick it up, and catch it in my left hand. I start walking to Julian's bedroom. I'm not going to let Siren stop me from killing him, not this time.

I'm sure Julian is awake after the commotion we made. And when I enter the dark bedroom, I no longer find him in the bed. My eyes scan the room, searching, but I don't find him. The snake is most likely hiding in his bathroom.

I start toward the bathroom, when Siren flips her body up, her legs throwing themselves around my neck and face, tightening hard, making it almost impossible to breathe.

"Drop the gun, sweetie," she says.

"Sweetie? Really?"

I can feel her smile even though I can't see it. "I'm sure

you've already called me every endearment in the book: sweetie, baby, lovely. That's what every man I fight usually does to try to make me feel inferior. You're no different."

I try to pull at her legs with my wounded hand, but her legs are much stronger than my bleeding hand.

"I. Would. Never. Call. You. Sweet," I say each word slowly, gasping for oxygen.

She bites down on the top of my ear, in both a harsh and seductive way.

Jesus, she's going to kill me while my dick is hard and begging for her. I'm not sure which is worse. Worse that she is strong enough to kill me, or that I'm going to die wanting her and never having her?

"Good, because I'm your siren. I'm not sweet; I'm not innocent. And I don't need a man to protect me."

Why are her words so sexy?

I can't pry her legs off me, but I can spin her around, so that's what I do—spin her until her pussy is at my face. I grin, knowing exactly how I'm going to get her to let go of my neck. Or she'll tighten her legs, and I'll die with her taste on my lips.

Either outcome is a win.

She's wearing tight jeans, but that isn't going to stop me. I may not be able to get to her skin, pussy, or clit directly, but I'll tease her enough through her jeans.

I open my mouth and groan into her pussy, biting down over her clit beneath her jeans.

She moans for a second before composing herself. "What are you doing?"

"Exactly what you want me to do."

She gasps when I lick and bite harder, slowly pulling all of her sex from her body as her pleasure soaks her jeans. Until I can taste the one part of her that is sweet.

I wait for her to release me. For her to jump off my face, with the need to attack and not let me control any part of her. But my tongue is magical when it comes to pussy, and she is a woman after all. She may not need a man for protection, but she needs a man for this.

When was the last time she was touched by a man before me?

From the way she's moaning and tightening her legs like a vice grip around my face, she at least wants my mouth and tongue.

And god do I want her too. But my teasing her is having the opposite effect to what I really need. I need to get her off of me so I can go kill Julian.

But when she moans, she makes it impossible to think of anything else. I want to rip her pants off and devour her properly. Then I want to throw her on the bed and fuck her slow and gentle, rocking her world in a way that she's not expecting, before I tie her up and fuck her hard against the wall like the seductress she is.

She pulls the scrunchie from my hair and runs her hand through my long locks. She refuses to let my head free as she pulls me tightly between her legs.

I bite down harder.

"Zeke!" she cries out.

Fuck me. Let me fuck you.

I don't think anymore as I pull at her shirt, needing skin, needing access to some uncovered part of her body.

I need her. It might have been a long time since Siren has been with a man, but it's been even longer since I've been with a woman—*too fucking long.* I've forgotten what it feels like to hear a woman scream my name.

Siren squirms against my legs, and I know she's getting close. I'm torn between denying her an orgasm and giving it to her just to hear her moan my name again.

But right now, all I can focus on is getting her to stop squirming. So I push her hard against a wall, trying to pin her body against my face.

Shattering glass corrects my perception of reality—I threw her against a window, rather than a wall. The window is too fragile to hold up against the force of our bodies slamming into it. I try to pull us back, to keep us inside, but my determination to fuck her with my mouth pushes our momentum forward.

We fall—our skin brushes harshly against broken glass as we fly through the window. Her legs automatically release my neck, and for a second, I feel free before I realize what is happening.

We are falling. Through a second-story window. We might not die if we hit the ground, but we will end up with many broken bones.

I drop the gun and grab onto the window sill with one hand. I reach for Siren's with the other, bloodied hand. Siren grabs on at the last second before our bodies slam into the side of the brick building.

We both breathe heavily as we realize how close to death we just came. How one moment of weakness together almost ended us both. We don't belong together. We just keep hurting each other.

"You okay?" I ask.

"No," she says.

But when I look down, I realize she's physically unharmed, but I can't get a good look at her face to tell what she's feeling.

"Climb up me," I say.

She hesitates for a second but then does as I say. I should climb up first and then pull her up. I don't trust her. As soon as she gets to the top, she could fling me to my death if she wanted to. But for some reason, I don't believe she will.

Siren climbs up my body, and then immediately turns around to extend her hand to me. I take it, and together we heave my giant body up. We both collapse onto the floor, exhausted. We're out of breath from the fighting, almost fucking, and then the almost tumbling to our deaths.

My hand reaches out automatically, needing to touch her to ensure that she is okay. Our fingers touch for the briefest of seconds; I can feel her pulse through her fingers. Rapid, quick, and in sync with mine.

His voice though breaks through any connection we have.

"Well done. Well done, pet," Julian says, using the nickname that he often calls her. He doesn't even show her enough respect to use her actual name—Aria. A name I can't bring myself to call her either. She'll always be Siren to me.

We both scramble to our feet, immediately sensing the danger.

"You can't beat my best asset. I pay Aria well to protect me," Julian says, standing by her side.

I fucking hate it. Moments ago, I was eating her out. I saved her life even when she was trying to destroy mine. And still, she chooses him instead of me.

"You only snuck out because she let you. It was all part of the plan. To seduce you and manipulate you into playing our game. The only way you leave is to play the game. Five rounds, and you can leave. Five rounds, and you are free."

I glare at Siren. I should have known she was manipulating me.

"Don't you get it? I will never play your game. I will never give up any information about my boss," I say.

Julian looks from me to Siren. "I think I can persuade you."

It happens so quickly that I don't even realize what he's doing. He grabs a piece of glass and then holds it to Siren's throat.

I take a step forward automatically but then stop. I need to stop showing how much I care about her. I shouldn't care.

"Play or I'll kill her," Julian says.

I shake my head. "You've already tried that. I don't care about her. Kill her."

"You lied to me before. And you're lying now. You care for her."

"So do you, which is how I know you won't actually kill her."

"I'll kill her if it gets you to play."

My heart beats wildly in my chest at the sight of a drop of blood that has formed on her neck. She told me not to save her. To save myself. *But can I really just stand here and watch her die?*

9

SIREN

I'VE NEVER FELT this afraid.

I've been through horrible things. I've faced death before, but every time I did, I was in control of my own body. I could fight back. I could save myself.

Julian has threatened to kill me before with the gun. But deep down, I didn't think he would actually do it.

This time, I can feel the sharp blade of glass in my neck. I can feel the blood beginning to spill. I can feel how just one slip would cause the edge of the glass to penetrate my artery instead of just my flesh.

But more importantly, I can feel Julian's heart beating against my back. I can feel the energy flowing through his body. And I know how much he's always wanted to do this. He's just been waiting for an excuse. Zeke is giving him that excuse.

But can I really just stand by and let Julian hold my fate in his hands? Let Zeke's answer decide if I live or die? All because of a contract I signed years ago?

No, I won't let these men hold my fate in their hands.

I always keep a weapon in my pocket. And while Julian

is distracted with Zeke, I grab the sharp knife in my back pocket, hidden from Zeke's view, and I silently move it against Julian's balls. He tenses as he realizes what I'm doing. I won't let him kill me, at least not without me castrating him first.

Julian tries to hold the glass tighter against my neck, but I press the end of the knife into his slacks. He loosens immediately until the glass is barely grazing my skin.

I stare at Zeke, trying to tell him not to play. Not to save me. I can save myself. Even though I know the consequences. I'll deal with them later.

From the glare Zeke is sending me, I don't think he plans on saving me. He thinks I planned this. That I seduced him and manipulated him into this very situation, forcing his hand to play the game.

I didn't.

But it makes no difference to Zeke. He will never trust me again.

"So what will it be? Play, or shall I kill Aria here?" Julian says, his voice surprisingly calm, considering where my knife is.

Zeke doesn't tear his gaze from me, and I wish he would. I've never seen him this angry before. My eyes drop to his bleeding hand—another injury I caused. I look at his leg, where his wound ripped open and is gushing blood. He's bleeding because of me. We both almost died because of me.

But god, does he have a magnificent tongue. I would have gladly died and gone through that window all over again just to feel his mouth between my legs.

I doubt Zeke feels the same way, though. He can't be mad for manipulating me when obviously he used my weakness, his mouth and tongue, against me.

"Last chance—are you playing my game or am I killing Aria?"

"I'll play. Not to save her. She deserves to die," Zeke says. His words cut through me worse than the glass against my neck. I didn't realize how much him wanting to protect me mattered to me. It stings to hear him say I deserve to die.

"I'll play because I want to be the one to kill you both. I'm tired of being manipulated. I'll play your game. I'll win. And before I get off this island, I'll kill you both," Zeke says.

Julian nods and drops the glass. I take a beat before I return the knife to my back pocket. I hear Julian breathe again for the first time in minutes.

"Aria will watch you then. We will play the first round tonight at dinner," Julian says, giving me a pointed look. A look instructing me to ensure Zeke's presence tonight, and warning me that he will deal with punishing me later for my little transgression with my knife.

"Why you aren't locking me back up in my cell?" Zeke asks.

"No, Aria is very capable of watching you. She'll do a better job than any bars. Dinner is at nine-thirty," Julian says, dismissing us before he pulls out his phone and yells at one of his maids to come clean up the glass.

Zeke turns and walks out without another word. I follow after.

For a man who is bleeding and injured, he's walking very quickly—not that I blame him. I want to get out of the house and as far away from Julian as possible too. Zeke didn't drive over, so we both walk the ten minutes back to Zeke's house. Neither of us talk or look at each other as we walk.

When we get to Zeke's house, I expect him to talk. Yell. *Something.*

Instead, he walks straight to his bedroom.

I sigh. I know he doesn't have any medical supplies to fix his wounds in there, so I run down to the basement to fetch the medical bag before heading to his bedroom. I pause in the doorway.

Zeke has his shirt off and has undone his pants, ready to remove them as well.

My mouth waters at his rippling muscles. And then I remember how soaked I still feel through my jeans where his mouth was devouring me only minutes before.

"Here—give me your hand and I'll stitch it up for you," I say, walking into his bedroom with the medical supplies.

Zeke growls, his body turning toward me with the force of a brick wall.

I stop dead in my tracks.

He snatches the bag from my hands with his uninjured hand. He doesn't speak, but he doesn't have to. It's obvious he doesn't want me to help him. Not only does he not want my help, but he won't allow it, even though it would be much easier for me to stitch him up than him trying with just one hand.

He's a stubborn man, so I'll let him try on his own first before doing it myself.

I take a deep breath and feel a sting at my neck. I look down and see blood flowing down onto my shirt. I need the medical kit too. But I won't beg for it. And if he won't accept my help, I won't accept his either. I can be just as stubborn. He once told me that seeing my pain hurts him as much as the physical pain hurts me. So I know he's hurting looking at me in pain.

At least, I hope he still is. Because I can't read any emotion in his eyes except anger.

"Out," Zeke commands.

I want to argue. I want to fight. But I'm tired of fighting. So instead, I turn and walk out.

"Truth or sin?" I hear Zeke ask as I get to the door.

I turn, afraid of what is going to come next.

"I should have let you die?" Zeke asks.

And for once, it's not a choice between giving him a sin or telling the truth. The truth is easy enough. "Yes."

He licks his lips. Drawing me to his mouth. Wanting a kiss. A whisper of his lips against my skin. A full-on attack of his lips and teeth on my body. *Anything*.

He smirks when he notices my reaction to the gesture. He's realized the power he has over me now. *Fuck*.

I open my mouth to ask my own truth or sin question. But before I can speak, he slams the door in my face. Leaving me bleeding, needy, and so god damned frustrated with him.

10

———

ZEKE

WHAT DO I do about Siren?

That's what keeps going through my head as I sit on the edge of the bed and pull out the supplies need to tend to my right hand. I try to work on stitching my hand, but I'm right-handed and struggle to get the needle to cooperate.

I drop the needle.

"Shit," I curse as I reach down on the floor, trying to find the needle. But it seems to have rolled under the bed.

My leg is throbbing.

My hand is burning.

And my chest is tight, exhausted from my near-death experience, and having conflicted feelings as I watched Julian hold the glass to Siren's neck.

I reach into the bag and pull out another needle. I drop it too.

"Fuck, fuck, fuck!" I scream as I kick the bag with my good leg.

The door to my bedroom flies open, and Siren runs in with determination and anger on her face. She may manipulate me with her feelings—pretending to want to fuck me—sometimes even liking me, but there is no doubt now that she hates me. She's not manipulating me; it's the truth.

"Stop being such a stubborn oaf and let me help you." She marches in and grabs the medical bag I flung across the room.

She picks it up and stomps over before kneeling in front of me; she grabs my hand without waiting for me to offer it up.

"Why would I ever let someone who manipulates and betrays me stitch me up?"

"Because you don't have any other option."

I try to pull my hand away, but she digs her fingers into my wound, and I wince and stop. Before she'd have been gentle—offered me drugs, taken care of me kindly. This time, I know she's going to enjoy every pierce of the needle.

And she does.

"That fucking hurts," I yell, as she digs into the palm of my hand.

"I know," she grins. "But that doesn't mean you can move. Stop wiggling."

"But it hurts!" I growl.

"Stop being a baby."

"I'm not being a baby. Do you have any idea how badly this hurts?"

She pushes the needle through my hand two more times, each eliciting a curse from me, before she finally finishes the stitching phase of caring for my wound.

"Yes, I do." She holds out her left hand, and I see a similar size scar to the one that will eventually form in my hand.

"How?" I ask, hating to see her in pain.

"It doesn't matter."

I sigh. *So many secrets, so many lies.* So many things I will never know about her.

She swallows, and the force of the movement pushes a few drops of blood out of her neck. Before, I thought the wound had stopped bleeding. It just looked like dry blood, but now, I can't focus on anything but the blood. On the pain Siren must be in.

She almost died today. Julian almost killed her to get to me. And I could have let him. Then he would have had nothing to hold over me. Nothing to get me to talk. Because everyone I love is safe as long as I don't talk.

I use my left hand to brush her hair off her neck and study the wound closer, but I can't see how deep it is while the blood is still flowing, and she's still working on cleaning my hand.

"Will you sit still so I can finish?" she demands.

"No," I growl back, ripping my hand from Siren's so I can examine her neck more closely.

She gasps at my movement and tries to fight to grab my hand again, but I'm determined now. I dig through the bag for some gauze and alcohol to clean the wound and dab the gauze with alcohol.

I grip her wrists in one of my hands as I clean her wound with the other. She hisses when the alcohol touches her skin.

My mouth moves to apologize for the pain she's in, but I stop myself. Instead, I just give her a glance to do the talking for me. My gaze must tell her everything my mouth wants to because she stops struggling enough for me to get a closer look at her neck.

I exhale a breath when I finally get a look at it.

"You don't need stitches. You'll have a nasty scar, but it's just a flesh wound," I say as I reach into the bag, pull out a bandage, and place it over her cut to stop the bleeding.

Siren doesn't say thank you; she just blinks her response. Finally, I release her, and she sits up, silently finishing bandaging up my hand.

The silence stretches until she is finished. And then she stands. "Be ready at nine-thirty," she says, as she walks to the door.

"Shouldn't I be ready before then if we are supposed to be at Julian's by nine-thirty?"

"No, arriving a few minutes late will allow you some control."

Or get me a bullet in my leg again. But I don't argue.

"You aren't going to stay and babysit me?"

She smiles, weakly. "No, I'm going to go take a bath. You won't run off. You protect those you love. Running would be selfish." And then she removes her shirt, tossing it on the floor as she starts heading toward the bathroom, no doubt leaving a trail of clothes behind her as she goes.

Leaving me hard, desperate, and feeling like I'm going to die if I keep spending time with her. Either from a lack of sex or a gunshot. Right now, I'd rather take the sex with the bullet than be alive and never get to fuck her.

At nine-thirty sharp, Siren reappears at my bedroom door. We haven't spoken or seen each other all evening, and the sight of her would knock me on my ass if I wasn't already sitting. She's wearing a simple black dress, with a high slit up the side and heels that make her legs look a million miles long. Her hair is down in long, wavy curls. Her makeup is simple yet striking. It's almost as if she isn't wearing any makeup except on her lips, drawing me to them so I can't think of anything but kissing her.

She's dressed for a night out, while I'm dressed as I always am—jeans and a T-shirt.

"I think I'm underdressed," I say.

She bats her eyes as a sultry smile spreads across her face. "No, you are wearing what is comfortable, same as me."

"That dress and those heels look anything but comfortable."

She shrugs. "You wear jeans as your armor, to be ready for a fight. I wear a dress when I need to feel more in control of the men around me."

Fuck, she's wearing the dress because she knows the reaction she will get from Julian and me. She's right. I won't be able to resist her all night. And neither will Julian. It gives her power. The cost is her being uncomfortable all night and not being able to run and escape in heels as easily.

Although, I'm sure she has plenty of weapons tucked away in various places in that dress. I can't imagine where she could fit any, though, with how tight and revealing that dress is.

"Well, I guess we are driving then," I say as I stand and look down at her heels.

She chuckles. "You don't think I'm as capable of walking in these heels as I am in flats?"

"Your skills constantly shock and surprise me, so I wouldn't put anything past you. But walking in those heels seems impossible."

"Just drive," she says, as we walk out of the bedroom and out to my truck.

The second I pull in front of Julian's house, the air between us changes. There is no more joking—no more appreciative glances. We will return to being enemies as soon as we walk in the door. Even if I don't understand why yet, Siren will stand by Julian's side.

We both walk up to the front door, which opens before we knock. One of Julian's men greets us.

"Mr. Reed is waiting for you in the dining room. Right this way, please," he says.

Siren no longer looks at me as we walk. She's all business. When we get to the dining room, and I see Julian sitting at the end of the table, I get flashbacks to the last time I was here. When Siren was tied up, when the men tried to touch her, when she fought back, only to be dragged up the stairs and...

I growl—the deepest, most ferocious sound I've ever made in greeting to Julian.

He just smiles and folds his hands across his lap.

"You're late," he says.

"I knew you'd wait," I say, not waiting for him to greet me and taking a seat next to him. Siren takes a seat across from me at the table, still not meeting my eyes.

Julian stares at Siren's neck, and then his gaze cuts down to her breasts. She does look incredible tonight. And I don't know what she did to cover the cut on her neck, but it's barely visible when she turns her head.

"Should we get to business then?" I say, wanting to get out of here as soon as possible.

Julian snaps his fingers, and a pair of servants strut in. One brings a bottle of wine and starts pouring, while the other carries soup.

Fuck, this is going to end up being a seven-course meal.

Julian starts talking, but it has nothing to do with our arrangement. I tune him out, trying to focus on the food in front of me when all of my attention is on how Julian looks at Siren and how he finds every excuse to touch her wrist. *And she fucking lets him.*

But when she laughs and leans in at one of Julian's jokes, I lose it.

I slam my glass of wine down on the table, causing the stem to break and red wine to spill onto the white table cloth. He should have served me whiskey, not wine to begin with, and maybe it wouldn't have happened.

All eyes turn to me.

"Ask your damn question already. I sat here and ate your food. If you want me to continue to sit here, then you will get on with why I'm here," I say.

Julian snaps his fingers again, and a servant enters, cleans up the broken glass, and then pours me a new one like nothing happened. But I notice that Julian is no longer touching Siren, so my outburst was worth it.

Julian takes his time drinking his wine like he's still working out how to play this.

"Really? You've had all evening and still haven't come up with the question you would like to ask me? You already know I won't give you any information, so the question is moot," I say.

"What is Enzo's Black main source of income?" Julian asks, narrowing his eyes as he studies me.

The question isn't that difficult. It wouldn't put Enzo in too much danger. With a little digging, Julian could figure out the answer anyway. But as I said, I will do nothing that harms my friends.

"I will never tell you the truth. I choose sin," I say, hoping like hell whatever he wants me to do won't destroy me. But I'm guessing whoever he wants me to hurt or attack is most likely his enemy. And if they are mixed up in this world, then they probably deserve whatever is coming their way.

Julian's eyes cut to Siren, and they exchange a silent conversation.

I try to study their relationship. *What are they saying? What are they thinking? How can they go from almost killing each other to quiet glances and conversations?*

Siren takes a deep breath, then she stands up and walks out of the dining room. Both Julian and I watch her ass as she walks away. She returns a moment later, holding a tablet. She flicks it on and then hands it to me.

I stare down at the screen filled with a picture of a man.

"I'll start you off with a simple task. One so simple that my Aria here could do it in her sleep," Julian says.

My eyes flick to Siren. I have no doubt she could do anything with ease. She is an expert temptress.

"He's a new player in the islands here. He's been buying up large stocks of weapons and persuading men I've worked with for years to change loyalty and work for him. I want him dealt with," Julian says.

Dealt with. I don't have to ask what he means by that. He wants me to find out who he is and then kill him. I don't know who this man is. I don't know if he is a good or bad man. But he's in this world. He knows the risks he takes every day. So if killing five men is the price I have to pay for ensuring Enzo and his family are safe, then I'll do it.

I stare down at the grainy picture. It's not a lot to go off of, so I hope Julian or Siren has more information to give me.

"What is his name?" I ask.

"Eli Beckett," Siren answers. "But that is all the information we have so far. Are you able to handle research, or do I need to find out more about him for you?"

I click off the image and give her a smirk. She has no idea what my life was like before I came here. Langston, my best friend, may have been better at discovering people who don't want to be found, but I have more skills than most. I'm sure Siren is capable, but so am I.

I stand up, not bothering to finish the steak or the rest of the food Julian had prepared.

"No, I think I can handle finding everything I need about Eli Beckett on my own."

I walk out without saying goodbye but pause when I hear Julian's voice. "Aria will ensure you stick to the task, instead of running away."

"I never run away from a deal," I say, glaring at Julian.

Siren gets up to follow me out, but Julian's voice impedes her. "I need a word with you first, Aria."

I storm back to the truck, intent on getting the fuck out of here and spending my night searching for Beckett. The sooner I can complete the five sins, the sooner I can leave this fucking island.

I don't bother waiting for Siren. "Siren can prove me wrong and walk back in her damn heels," I grumble under my breath, not wanting to deal with her right now.

But when I get back to the house, I don't storm to my laptop to search for Beckett. Instead, I find myself in the kitchen, drinking a glass of whiskey, waiting for her.

About thirty minutes later, I hear the front door open. She doesn't even bother to knock. I plan on reaming her out and then spending my night alone.

But as soon as I catch a glance at Siren's thigh from her dress hiking up her leg when she walks into my kitchen, I decide on a very different way to spend my night.

"I'm going to sleep. Let me know if you need any help

with your research," Siren says, starting to walk through the house.

I grab her hand, stopping her in her tracks as our hands' touch. And then I spin her around, electricity blasting through us.

"I never got to finish my sin."

"Didn't you?"

"No, our kiss was only the beginning."

11

SIREN

I SHUDDER as Zeke whispers in my ear, his voice bringing me back from where my mind has gone. I've been locked on my conversation with Julian after our drawn out dinner.

I exhale deeply, trying to push Julian out of my head and body. I just want to go to bed. Tomorrow I can face Julian, Zeke, and whatever else tomorrow brings.

"I need to sleep, Zeke. I'm tired," I say. Before dinner, I would have jumped his bones. I would have done anything for him to fuck me. To steal another kiss or two. And connect our bodies in a tangled dance of sweat and desire to release an explosion inside both of us.

But now, after Julian—well, I just can't.

Julian might have realized we would come back and fuck. He probably said what he said, and did what he did, because he knew I wouldn't be able to after...

"Siren?" Zeke says.

I blink rapidly and look at him.

"Yes?"

He studies me a moment, in the careful way he does, which feels like he's glimpsing into my soul. But of course, he can't. He doesn't know my truth any more than I know his.

"Whiskey or wine?" he asks. He doesn't give me the option to turn him down.

I sigh. "Whiskey." I've had enough wine after our dinner. I follow Zeke to the kitchen, where I've restocked the fridge and liquor cabinet. He goes to work pouring us both a glass. All I want to do is kick off my blister-forming shoes and unpeel myself from this dress.

"Thanks," I say as I take the offered glass. I'm very careful not to let our fingers brush as I take it.

Zeke's lip twitches as he notices how cautious my movement was. If his plan was to slowly seduce me, it's not going to work.

We both slowly sip our whiskey.

"I should get to bed. It's been a long day," I say.

"I agree we should go to bed," he says.

My heart stops at his voice, and a jolt hits me between my legs. *Why does his voice have to be so sexy?*

"Separate beds," I clarify.

He frowns. "There is only one bed in this house, unless you count the one in the basement, but I doubt you'll want to sleep there."

"Care to be a gentleman and sleep on the couch?"

He downs his drink. "I'm no gentleman, Siren."

Siren, I love it when he calls me that. I know he means it as an insult, but when he says it, it never comes across that way. He doesn't say it in the same harsh way he says Julian's name. Zeke calls me Siren like it's a term of endearment.

Zeke places his glass on the counter, and then he starts walking toward the bedroom, but I can still feel his heated eyes on me. His words still reverberate through my core. I remember how his lips felt against mine, kissing me like I am the only thing in his world he cares about.

I want that again.

But I can't have it.

It's not mine to take.

I rub my neck; the fresh scar there clearly reminding me who I really am—a siren. Not Zeke's Siren; I'm a real monster. And I won't mix business with pleasure. At least, not again.

I shouldn't follow Zeke to the bedroom. I should stay out here and surrender to sleeping on the couch. But I never do what I *should* do. I'm a slow learner.

I walk into the bedroom and watch as Zeke kicks off his shoes, preparing for bed like he didn't just promise to commit a sin with me. *Why did I think of that stupid game anyway?* I could have gotten the same number of answers out of Zeke without having to play a game that causes me to lose every time.

I stare at the big bed. We've slept in it plenty of times before; we can sleep in it again without fucking each other's brains out.

Yes, that's all we are going to do—sleep.

Zeke grabs the back of his shirt and begins pulling it one-handed over his head in the way all men know how to do. As it inches higher, my eyes zoom in on every muscle I will never get to feel, every tattoo I will never get to explore, every piece of skin I won't get to add my own mark to.

And then he starts unzipping his pants, and I force my eyes away. I can't look at him. I won't fuck him. Not tonight, not *ever*.

I turn around and start messing with the zipper on the back of my dress, just needing out of these tight clothes and into bed as soon as possible. I don't even care about grabbing a shirt to slip on first; I just want to get in that bed where I can pretend to sleep.

"Here, let me help you," Zeke says when I fidget with the zipper again. I can't get it to move even an inch down.

I relent wordlessly. *He's helping you unzip; he's not undressing you,* I tell myself.

I feel his fingers against my back, and then he moves to my hair to sweep it off my neck.

I still, afraid he's going to discover one of my secrets, but if he does, he doesn't say anything. And if Zeke found my secret, he most definitely would speak up.

I hold my breath, feeling his tantalizing fingers brush against the skin on my back as he works my zipper down, down, down...

Down past the point where I can easily finish the job myself. Past the point where he's simply being a helpful gentleman. But then again, he's already told me he isn't a gentleman. I feel him stop just above the curve of my ass, and I have no doubt he would have continued if the zipper went lower.

He doesn't speak.

I finally exhale when his hands are no longer on my body. I don't dare turn around.

I grab the straps of the dress and lower them before shimming the dress down over my hips until it falls to the floor. I'm not wearing a bra; there was no way to wear one with this dress. So just my thong underwear keeps me decent. I'm still wearing my heels, needing to feel powerful and strong up until the last moment before hitting the bed.

The bed is behind me, and Zeke is standing between it and me. I could walk backward to the bed, and he wouldn't see my naked breasts. Although, he's seen them before and I'm not a shy woman. I should prance over like I know how much my body affects him. But I can't because the problem isn't him—*it's me.*

I can't turn around and strut to the bed without looking at him. Him shirtless, possibly pantless. No matter what happened before, I'm still a woman. A woman with needs that haven't been met in a very long time.

I can't.

I shouldn't.

It's wrong.

But I know what's going to happen before I even turn around. It was inevitable. Everything has been leading to this. And we can't move on until it happens.

Then we can move on...

We can have one electric, passionate moment together. Like a storm blowing through town. Something that can never be repeated because the same storm conditions literally can't converge again.

I close my eyes, trying to steady my breath and heart. My heart is what I'm most worried about. I don't fall in love easily, or anything close to it. But Zeke isn't a typical man. He's capable of tricking my heart into confusing lust with love. And I need to constantly remind my heart that Zeke feels no such love for me.

He hates me. He can never love me. My heart needs to stay steady, strong, and unswayed by his body.

I brush my hair back around my neck with my hands and wince at the feeling. I hated what happened with Julian before I left dinner, but right now, it's the perfect reminder. A reminder that is going to get me to walk into the bed without letting Zeke's naked body tempt me.

I turn.

I walk.

I stop.

Fucking Zeke.

He's standing, in just his boxers, with a damn smirk on his lips and heat in his eyes. The kind of cocky arrogance that says he's about to get what he wants.

I want to deny him just to wipe the smugness from his face.

But his arrogance is earned.

I stand taller, pushing my breasts out as I do, my nipples hardening under his appreciative stare. He rakes over my body, and it's like he's telling each part of my body exactly what he plans on doing. How he will kiss, lick, nibble on my body. How he plans to pull scream after scream from my throat. How he plans to give me orgasm after orgasm.

He won't beg. He won't ask. And he won't force me.

He's making it clear that this is my choice. That if I say yes, he will take control. And I'll have no control left. No power. I will give it all to him. And I don't know in the morning light if I'll be able to get it back.

He thinks he's gaining control in this moment. But I know the trick to retaining power. And it's giving it up willingly. Because you are confident in getting it back. Or you don't care about power in the first place.

"Yes," I say, my voice soft yet strong.

A switch changes in Zeke, and it takes everything in him not to attack me at full speed.

I move to kick my heels off, needing something to do—one last moment of self-possession.

"Leave them on," Zeke says in his deep husky voice.

I do. And I know right here, right now that I want Zeke to have complete dominance over me. I know that if I surrender to him, if I do exactly what he says, I will have one of the best nights of my life. And I need a night where I don't have to think. I can let someone else do that for me. I can let someone else worry about pleasure and pain, right and wrong.

Zeke smiles when I leave my heels on.

"So you can obey," he says.

"Only when I want to."

"And what do you want right now, Siren?"

"You."

That's all it takes—one word. He grabs my neck, pulling me to his hard chest and exquisite lips, the pain he's causing my neck is undeniable, but I don't care the second our lips crash and our tongues tangle. All I feel is Zeke. And it's more than enough to spin my entire world on its axis.

I kiss back hard, my tongue pushing and pulling and begging for everything I need tonight to be. I don't think about all the harm I'm doing. I only think about how good this feels.

I don't think I've ever been so selfish as I'm going to be with Zeke. But I want to be selfish. Tomorrow I'll deal with the consequences.

"Don't think this is going to be anything but a sin," Zeke says against my lips as his hand runs down the side of my body, feeling every curve.

"A euphoric sin—I can live with that," I say.

More hot, breathy kisses follow. The kind that push us so close to the edge of reason that we could come under attack by burglars, a tornado could rip through the room, and a hurricane could breeze through—none of it would stop us because we are incapable of stopping. The animalistic need we have for each other has taken over. Nothing will get in the way—not this time.

Zeke growls, and I prepare for the storm. But nothing can prepare me for anything this man does.

He grabs my body and flips me over the bed, until my

face is on the bedspread and my ass in the air. He kicks my legs apart and leans over my back until I can feel his hot breath on my neck.

"This is my sin, not yours. If I could enjoy you without you feeling anything, I would. But it's impossible for me to fuck you without you feeling pleasure."

I gasp as his teeth bite down on my ear; it's both too gentle and too hard.

I squirm underneath him at the intoxicating way his body gets mine ready for everything he has planned. I already know I'm dripping and more than ready for him, even though I know he's huge from the outline in his underwear. My body wants it all—now. It demands it.

"Where is it?" he asks, panting but no longer kissing or teasing me. For a split second, he's found a way to be back in the real world instead of the storm we've created.

"Where's what?" I ask, forcing the words out.

"Your weapon. You always have one on you."

I smirk, biting my lip. *Smart man.*

"The only place it could be when I'm only wearing a thong."

He kisses my neck, tormenting me as he reaches into my underwear between my butt cheeks and pulls out the knife I forgot I tucked away there. It's why I hate wearing dresses, the places to hide weapons are so much more inconvenient than when wearing jeans.

I hear the sound of the knife hitting the floor. "I don't know how you're able to walk around knowing one wrong move could mean the knife will slice into your body."

I smile and then turn my head, giving him a small wink. "I get off on pain."

And then I get the reward I was looking for. His eyes

widen to extraordinary heights. His mouth drops open. And for a moment, I have power again.

But then he slaps my ass, blurring the lines between rough and blissful. And I know I'm about to pay for my split second of control.

"Cameras?" he asks, his ability to speak becoming less and less.

"Door, light fixture, dresser."

He stands up, giving me a moment to breathe. "Dresser?"

"Mmm-hmm," is all I can get out. The door and light fixture are obvious. I always hide one camera in an unlikely place even if it doesn't get the best audio or visuals, it's least likely to be found.

I hear him moving quickly to destroy each of the cameras, but I don't move even though the position is an uncomfortable one. I want to be ready as soon as he finishes to continue on right where we left off.

Zeke moves a little too fast with the light fixture, and instead of just pulling the camera off, I hear a loud crash, and I know the fixture is coming down, right on top of me.

I scramble to climb up the bed, but I won't make it. Gravity moves faster than I do when I'm needy and under Zeke's intoxication.

But instead of the sharp glass, I feel Zeke's heavy body land on top of mine.

We both breathe hard. This isn't the first time we've ended up in a position like this.

"Stop saving me," I say, my voice angry, and my desire slowly departing my body.

"I didn't."

"Then why are you lying on top of me, your back most likely scratched with glass, while I'm uninjured?"

He yanks mercilessly on my hair, and I hear sparks of electricity fly overhead. *Or is it us?* I can't tell anymore.

"Because if you got hurt, then I couldn't do this." He kisses me savagely. And this time, I know a falling chandelier won't stop us. Not even if it caught the room on fire.

I moan as his kisses turn carnal, and I feel his erection press against my ass. I'm sure he's bleeding, but I don't care. I want this. *I need this.* And he does too.

We might both be injured, but we are fucking.

Now.

I need more.

I start turning underneath him. Needing to feel his skin, touch his cock, rake my eyes over my body.

"You aren't in control, Siren," Zeke says into my ear. "Not tonight."

The room has gone dark without the light fixture. So I can barely make him out as he digs through his dresser, I assume to get a condom. A second later, I see the flicker of light as he turns the lamp on.

He wants to see me when he fucks me, not remain in the dark.

I smile. *I want to see him too.*

But then I see what he grabbed—two ties. I won't be seeing much of Zeke after all. He's going to ensure I get as little pleasure out of this as possible, just like he said.

"Wrists," Zeke says, all business-like.

I extend my arms out in front of me. He takes one of the ties and binds my wrists together. I've been with men who are into kinky shit before, but I don't think that's what it is with Zeke. He just wants me to not be able to touch him. He wants to deny me the pleasure of running my hands through his hair or across his chest.

And then he does the thing that hurts even worse. He

wraps the second tie around my eyes so I won't be able to see him.

Sure, my other senses will be heightened. I'll be able to feel more than I would have before. But I won't be able to see Zeke's body. Won't be able to see his cock when he enters me. Won't be able to see the expressions he makes when he comes. I deserve to only get one part of him, not the whole package.

I swallow hard, waiting for Zeke to make his move.

And what a move it is.

In one movement, he's ripped my panties from my body, and his face his buried between my ass cheeks, his tongue lapping between my legs.

I get flashbacks to the last time his tongue licked my clit, bringing me one of the best orgasms of my life. But tonight isn't about my pleasure, so I don't expect him to give a repeat performance.

"What are you doing?" I ask, because I can't help myself.

"Making you wet."

"I'm already wet." I may want his tongue, but I'm desperate for his cock. As soon as he slides in, I'll come; I'm that close to coming.

Zeke's tongue flicks, finding my clit even though my ass and folds should be blocking his way. He finds it, knowing exactly what I want.

I moan as my teeth dig into the sheets to keep from screaming. He shouldn't affect my body this quickly. But god, a few more seconds, and I'll be screaming, crying, and exploding all at the same time. *Man, does he know how to work his tongue.*

"Zeke, stop I'm going to—"

"Come, Siren," Zeke commands.

"But...I want..." *I want to come on his dick.* If I come now, I'm not sure I'll be able to come a second time so quickly.

"Come now, Siren. I want you drenched and ready for my cock."

Damn, if I wasn't about to come before, I'm ready now.

I come.

I try to keep from screaming his name. I try to keep some dignity, some control. But he pushes one of his fingers in, expertly curling it against my G spot. And I've lost all control.

"Zeke Kane," I scream, as my arms buck and throb needing to touch him. My eyes yearn to see him. I don't get either, though. But his grin between my legs is enough.

I pant heavily as I come down off my high. It was exhilarating, but my throbbing pussy is clearly more than ready for round two.

Zeke kisses up my ass, then up my lower back.

I smile, content and excited about what comes next. I'm so lost in my bliss that I don't even realize what Zeke is doing until it's too late.

He grabs my hair, fisting it into a ponytail as his cock presses against my ass. He may have made me come with his tongue, but he's going to take me from behind, making it all about sex and nothing else.

But the second his hand grabs onto my hair, he stops. And I know exactly what's stopping him.

Fuck.

Thank god I can't see Zeke because I'd probably lose it. I'd get angry or go right back to what Julian did to me before I left his house. I haven't seen the mark he left on my neck, but I doubt it's a pretty sight.

Zeke releases my hair with a curse, and then I feel him leave the bed.

What the?

I wait for a second. Then another.

What's happening? Is he really not going to fuck me? Is he going to let Julian win again?

"Zeke?" I whisper, feeling more alone than I've felt in a while.

He doesn't answer.

But then I feel the bed sink. I feel my hair being pulled high in a ponytail as he ties it up with a scrunchie. The burn of my neck eases as it does. And then I feel him press a bandage over the scars, covering the mark.

"Does it hurt anymore?" Zeke asks.

"No," I answer. "I don't feel anything when I'm with you." And now that Zeke's removed my hair from my neck and bandaged the scar, it feels numb. But I'm not sure it's enough to get Zeke to fuck me. Not after he saw what Julian did.

My fears are proven right when I feel Zeke loosening the tie around my eyes. It drops away, and I try to hide my disappointment.

He flips me over. He's still naked, still between my legs, but I know this isn't happening anymore. And I won't beg.

My eyes slowly climb up his body until I see his pupils.

"You may be loyal to Julian, but tonight you're mine. I don't want you to forget that," Zeke says.

I don't belong to anyone. But I don't say the words out loud. Because they would be a lie. For the first time, I want to belong to a man. At least, I want to belong in his bed. I want him to know exactly how to get me off, exactly what I need without me having to ask for it.

"Don't close your eyes, not for a second," he commands.

I nod, unable to speak.

This is still happening.

I let my eyes devour all of his body. *Remember this forever. It won't ever happen again.*

I stop at his cock, now on full display, and my lips part in shock. It's huge, just like the man kneeling over me.

He smirks at my expression. "You said you got off on pain. Let's test that theory."

I bite my lip, trying not to worry. *No wonder he made sure I came first.* There was no way he was fitting without me completely turned on and soaked.

He spreads my legs as he moves closer.

"Pill?" he grunts as he moves in, resting his cock over my slit.

I nod. "Clean?"

He nods.

We are going to fuck without a condom. *Reckless?* Definitely. *Worth it?* Abso-fucking-lutely.

He pushes my still tied arms back over my head, causing my back to arch and my breasts to move closer to him.

He leans over, blowing on my nipples gently until they are pointed into sharp peaks just for him. His tongue touches one, teasing and tasting until all I can think about is his tongue.

I'm lost in his tongue, until I feel the unfamiliar stretch as he pushes deep inside me.

Oh, my god.

I can't breathe.

My heart has stopped.

All I can do is stretch as I adjust to him inside me.

It's everything I expected it to be, feeling his intrusion: wrong, painful, and jolting. And it's everything I didn't expect: right, delicious, and intoxicating.

"You with me?" he asks, his voice strained.

"Yes," I pant.

"Good, because I'm not even half-way in, baby."

Holy fuck.

He moves, somehow getting deeper. My eyes water a second as he hits deeper than any man has ever reached inside me. As long as he comes nowhere near my heart, I know I'll be okay. I'll recover from this.

And then he tenderly kisses me. So softy compared to how hard the rest of his body is.

I melt.

Into goo.

My body opens, allowing him all the way in.

And then his hand caresses my neck. *Mine*—his eyes say.

I don't argue. He's right. *I'm his.* At least for tonight.

Then he grips my ponytail.

"Ready?" he asks.

I nod, although I know I'll never be ready for what he has to give.

He pulls out almost completely, and then he thrusts. His pelvis, that part that forms a perfect V, rubs against my clit as he dips all the way inside me. He somehow hits every nerve ending in my body as he thrusts.

All pain leaves. My body is his to do what he wants with.

He thrusts over me, pounding into my body with everything he has. Each thrust more beautiful and delicious than the previous.

And I get to see it all. The way his body moves expertly over mine like he already knows exactly what my body wants and needs. The way his brow furrows with sexy determination. The ways his lips curl. The way his muscles flex with each movement.

We are both getting close to the explosive end. The release we have both been chasing. And then this will all be over. Every sexually charged conversation will be over. The intensity between us will leave when our orgasms hit, and this will all become a faint memory.

My arms twitch above my head. I got my sight back, but Zeke won't let me feel him. No matter how desperate I am to be as connected to him as possible. I want to feel him and kiss him when we both come.

Zeke leans down again as he keeps pumping into me. Until his lips are kissing mine again, giving in to one of my wishes.

"Dig your heels into my back," he says.

I do, and god the movement pushes him deeper inside me. I'm going to come, I'm so close.

"Wrap your arms around my neck," he says.

Shock.

I did not expect that kindness.

But I don't question it. I loop my arms around his neck, allowing me to feel his long hair with my fingers as he gives me everything—kisses, connection, and the most earth-shattering orgasm known to man.

"Zeke!" I scream.

"Siren!"

Our voices tangle together, just like our bodies. I feel the warmth of his cum as it fills me. I've never been fucked without a condom before. I've also never fucked a man who wasn't just a man, but my enemy as well.

Slowly, our bodies come back to earth, but Zeke doesn't pull out of my body. And I don't move or squirm beneath him. I want this to last as long as possible.

"Tomorrow, we return to enemies. This was my last sin when it comes to you. But I promise you this; I will kill Julian. So if I were you, I'd reconsider who you're loyal to. He's a dead man for what he did to your neck alone. Choose who you are loyal to carefully. Because if you choose Julian, I'll ruin you too."

And then he pulls out, leaving me empty and alone.

He doesn't realize it doesn't matter who I'm loyal to. Zeke already ruined me. He may not have left a physical mark on my body like Julian did, but Zeke left a different kind of scar. A mark that no amount of time will ever heal. A permanent stain on my soul.

12
———

ZEKE

FUCKING SIREN WAS everything I always imagined it would be.

Pulling out of her broke me.

Because it was the first time and the last time.

It should be the first of a million times, but I meant what I said. We are enemies. This was a momentary slip in judgment. It was sin in every meaning of the word. I shouldn't have fucked her. I'll never be able to fuck a woman again without thinking about her. But I couldn't *not* fuck her. Even when I saw what Julian did to her.

Why the hell is she still loyal to him? He hurt her, so many times. I may not be able to make Siren loyal to me, but I've decided one thing—my mission now includes making her see that Julian Reed does not deserve her allegiance. I might even convince her to be the one to put a bullet in his head.

I get off the bed, and the second my feet hit the floor, I know this moment is over. I walk over to the dresser and pull out a T-shirt and boxers. I slip the boxers on and carry the T-shirt to Siren, who still lays on the bed with her wrists tied together. It's clear from her expression that she is no longer present. Her mind is somewhere else.

I grab her wrists and pull her into a sitting position, forcing her to look at me. Then I remove the tie and slip the shirt over her head and arms. I pull her feet into my lap and remove the shoes she dug into my back. Finally, I grab the remnants of the fallen light fixture and toss it off the bed.

"Let me see your back," she says.

I turn, letting her see that I'm not hurt before I sit down on the edge of the bed next to her.

"Why? Why are you loyal to Julian? Why did he brand your neck?"

She swallows hard. I don't expect her to answer. But she does. And I realize it's because there are no cameras for Julian to hear her.

"I'm not loyal to him. I'm loyal to myself. Trust me when I say that the only reason I do what Julian asks is for my own selfish reasons. And the second following him no longer serves my interests, I'll kill him myself."

I blink rapidly, not believing her words.

"It's the truth. I don't lie, remember? At least not with my words."

"Why do you put up with him hurting you?"

"I don't."

I frown. "Your neck, leg, and every other scar on your body prove otherwise."

She sighs and pulls her legs up to her chest and wraps her arms around them.

"You didn't deserve to have him carve a JR into your neck."

"Is that what he did?" she asks, her eyes bulging for a second.

Maybe if she sees what he did, realizes how bad of a

man he is, she'll change her loyalty. I jump off the bed and then grab her hand, pulling her with me. I take her to the bathroom, remove the bandage I placed on her neck, and hand her a small mirror. She takes her time holding up the handheld mirror and positioning it so she can see the back of her neck where Julian carved his initials—initials she will never be able to remove.

"Help me kill him," I say.

She frowns, blinking rapidly. And I realize there are cameras in this room. She won't speak against him here.

"Look what he did to you," I snarl.

She does, and I see the pain in her eyes. I don't know if I've ever met a stronger woman—Kai maybe, a woman who flipped my boss's world upside down. But Siren has something that Kai doesn't have—skills. She knows how to shoot a gun. She knows how to fight. She could easily fight her way out of this situation. She doesn't need me to save her.

But it's clear from her eyes that she won't fight Julian. I just don't know why.

"You think he got away without me hurting him?"

"Yes."

She shakes her head and then looks past me, I assume to a camera. "I've hurt Julian worse than he will ever hurt me. I'm not faithful to him. And one day, when I no longer need him, I'll kill Julian Reed." Her eyes go back to me. "Until then, my job is to ensure you complete your five sins since I know you will never tell him a truth. Get some sleep, Zeke. Tomorrow we go hunt down a man."

And then she walks out, leaving me more confused than ever. She's the most confusing, irritating, strong, fragile, infuriating woman I've ever met.

But at least I learned one thing—she hates Julian Reed as much as I do. She may not have told me the complete truth yet. Julian has something on her; that's why she follows his orders. And someday, he will hurt her badly enough that she will flip. She'll stop doing his bidding.

I'm close to figuring out what that breaking point is. And when I do, she'll be mine.

13

SIREN

I shouldn't have said it. I shouldn't have spoken such truths out loud. Not when I knew Julian was listening. It was reckless of me.

But who am I kidding? Julian already knew I want him dead. I may never have spoken the words out loud, but I've spoken them enough in my mind. If Julian Reed ever stops being useful to me, I'll kill him.

There is only one little problem with that truth—Julian Reed will never stop being useful to me. He will never stop holding my life in his hands. I will never kill Julian; he knows that. Zeke doesn't. But Zeke deserved to learn how I felt. He deserved to know that he isn't the only person who hates Julian.

I pull the throw blanket up, tight under my chin as I curl up on the couch. I should be sleeping in Zeke's bed. Possibly even tucked against his naked body, praying that when he wakes up, we would get a round two.

Instead, I'm alone lying on the couch in Zeke's living room, trying to forget about how swollen my lips are from his kisses and how sore my body is in all the right places. Even though I finally got my wish, I got to fuck Zeke, I'm still horny and turned on and feel like I could explode from his touch. Fucking Zeke didn't get him out of my system; it just made me crave him more.

I close my eyes, forcing Zeke out of my head. Tomorrow I have a job to do. And the faster Zeke completes the five sins he owes Julian, the faster he will be out of my life for good, and my life can return to the way it was before.

Sleep pulls me under quickly, but even sleep can't protect me from my demons…

———

"A word, Siren," Julian says as Zeke walks out of the dining room.

I stay.

I pick up my glass of wine and take a long sip, watching Zeke walk away from me.

"Come here," Julian says as he continues to sit at the end of the table.

I hate being summoned, being treated like a dog. But I choose my battles when it comes to Julian. And this isn't one I want to fight. *Just get this over with so I can go after Zeke.*

I doubt he waited for me, though. I'm going to have to walk back to his house in these damn heels. Zeke was right, heels suck and are almost impossible to walk in, even if they make me feel powerful for a few minutes.

I slide my chair out, keeping my wine glass in my hand as I walk over to Julian.

He pats his lap, telling me to sit there.

I frown. "Really?"

He raises his eyebrows. "Are you going to defy me, again?"

The way Julian says 'again' tells me everything I need to know. He's pissed, and I don't have to think too hard to know why—he's angry I put a knife to his balls, when I swore I'd never hurt him, never use my skills against him.

That stupid vow.

"Sit, Aria," Julian says.

Everything inside of me falls heavily as I sit on his lap, completely defeated. I don't know why I fight against Julian. He always wins. *He will always win.*

I'm surprised to not feel his erection poking me in the ass when I sit. At least I have that to be thankful for.

Julian continues to glare at me, and it's clear my punishment won't stop at just sitting on his lap.

"You broke your vow," he says.

I nod, not defending myself.

"You know the consequences of breaking the vow."

Pain stings my heart. *No, please no.*

"I do. I'm sorry," I say, hating that I'm apologizing to this man.

"Are you? Because I don't think you are sorry at all, Aria."

I'm not. He knows I'm not. I wish I had the guts to slice his balls clean off. But I couldn't...I can't.

"You beat me up, you shot me, threatened to kill me. What was I supposed to do? Let you kill me?"

"Yes."

I scowl. "Well, you should have known I would never let you do that without putting up a fight."

His lips curl just a little. *That was his plan.* He knew I couldn't not fight back. He goaded me.

I slap him.

I watch his face turn shocked. I watch the redness spread across his face. And it's worth every punishment he's about to deal out.

But when his head turns back to me, I realize I've just made a horrible mistake.

"You broke your vow, again," he says.

"Consider my vow over. I quit," I say, moving to get up off his lap.

"Really? You might want to reconsider."

I gasp when I see the glint of evil in his eyes. I want to take it all back. *Everything.* Because I know exactly what Julian is thinking and I can't—I just can't. I can't do this again...

"I'm sorry," I whisper, trying to hold back my tears. And I am truly sorry. He has no idea how sorry I am.

"Prove it," he says.

I close my eyes, taking a deep breath as I try to think of something that will make Julian trust me again. Something that will prove I'm still on his side. That I will always be on his side. Because I can't live with the consequences.

I feel Julian's excitement grow in his slacks. I could fuck him...*No, I couldn't.*

There is only one option—*make another vow.*

I grab the steak knife on the table and hand it to him.

He smiles as I do.

Then I lift my hair, exposing my neck to him. "I vow—"

And then I feel the slice of the blade through my neck. And no matter what words leave my mouth, I promise myself that someday I'll be free of Julian Reed. Even if it's only in death.

———

My eyes flutter open as I'm soaked in sweat and fear. *Julian's not here. It was just a nightmare.*

But I feel eyes on me. I look up and see Zeke watching me with a frown on his face. He's leaning against the doorframe, shirtless, and wearing gray sweatpants that are somehow sexier than if he were wearing nothing at all. *What is it about gray sweatpants?* I ignore the bulge in his pants and focus on the scowl.

"What are you doing here?" I ask.

"You were talking and screaming in your sleep. It woke me up."

"Sorry, I didn't mean to wake you." I sit up, tucking my knees to my chest. I'm wearing Zeke's T-shirt, and the smell of him alone comforts me. But what I really want is for Zeke to wrap his big, tattooed arms around me. Tell me everything is going to be okay. That he'll protect me. But I've lost Zeke's protection. I'm not his friend; I'm his enemy.

I replay the nightmare in my head. Zeke said I was talking.

"What did I say?" I ask, not sure if I hope he heard everything or nothing at all.

"The truth."

"Which is?"

Zeke doesn't answer. But the unnerving frown on his face tells me enough. Whatever he heard made him furious. At me. At Julian. At the world.

"I'll try not to wake you again," I say, moving to pull the throw blanket back over me and attempt to sleep again. *Like that's going to happen.*

"Come to bed," he says. It's a command. I hate commands, except maybe when Zeke commands me. There is something sexy and protective about how he orders me to do something. And right now, I don't want to sleep alone, even if sleeping in Zeke's bed complicates things.

So I follow Zeke to the bedroom. I climb under the covers, as does Zeke, and then I close my eyes, hoping I will be able to sleep better with Zeke nearby to chase my nightmares away.

I feel the dip of the bed as Zeke moves closer. And then I feel his arms wrap around me tightly. I smile, knowing I won't have another nightmare. But I also know I'm completely fucked as my heart flutters in my chest.

Zeke isn't mine. And I can't be his.

Fucking him might have been enjoyable, and telling him I want to kill Julian may have proven to Zeke that we are closer to being on the same side than he realizes, but in the end, I know my fate—and it will require me to betray Zeke, again.

14

ZEKE

"I vow…"

Those were the words that Siren said in her sleep, trembling, and lost in a nightmare. It took everything in me just to listen and not wake her up. I couldn't stand to just stand by when I could do something to stop her suffering. But Siren is a closed book when it comes to her relationship with Julian. There is something big I'm missing, something she's not telling me. So I forced my legs to stay still, to not move toward her.

But I'm not sure it was worth it because I got so little for my effort—*I vow*.

Two words with so much meaning.

The only people who typically say vows are brides and grooms getting married.

Are Siren and Julian married?

My heart beats erratically at that thought. Siren is currently using my shoulder as a pillow. Her leg is draped over mine, and her heart rests against my chest beating in sync with my own. I'm afraid my beating heart will be enough to wake her up, but she doesn't move.

I stare down at her left hand. No ring, no tan line, no sign she's married to that monster. *She's not married to Julian.* He wouldn't let her fuck me if she was. He wouldn't let her be sold to me knowing what most men would do to her once they bought her. And the kicker is that I've asked Siren before if she was married and she said no. *She always tells the truth.* And so far, she has.

Except when she's convincing me of a lie, I think. But I heard her say the words; she's not married to Julian Reed. I just don't know what vow she promised him. *What loyalty does he demand of her?*

I run my hand through Siren's hair. *What would I give to make her mine?*

I know the answer, but I won't even allow myself to think it. She's not mine. She will never be mine. She's my enemy. She betrayed me, and she'll do it again if it pleases her. When I've finished my five sins, I'll be gone, and she'll stay here by Julian's side. She might as well be married to him.

I can't keep lying here in this bed dreaming about what a life with Siren could be. There is no could be, might be, or even currently is with us. Because there is no us. It was just sex. Breathtaking, fantastic sex that can never be repeated. I shouldn't even have let her into my bed except I knew I wouldn't be able to sleep if I didn't fuck her.

But there is no reason I still need to be in bed now.

I jump out, not caring if she wakes up, and head to the shower. In the shower, I can wash away all thoughts of last night. I can wash away Siren's scent on my body. I can wash away *her.*

So that's what I do. I force my mind to change from thoughts of Siren to this Eli Beckett guy I'm supposed to hunt down and kill. I've done countless tasks like this for Enzo

Black before. I can do this in my sleep. I decide to take a boat over to St. John, the neighboring island where Beckett was last spotted and start there. On my way over, I'll do an extensive background check on our Eli Beckett, but I can't use any of my usual resources. I don't want any of my friends to know where I am; it would put their lives in danger. And it would be easier for Julian to track them down. I'll have to use backchannels.

I start rinsing the shampoo from my hair when the bathroom door pops open and Siren struts in. She's changed, no longer wearing just my T-shirt. She's now wearing jeans with flats, and she's tied my T-shirt up so it stops just below her breasts and exposes her stomach. Her hair is pulled in a high ponytail, and she's wearing a modest amount of makeup. She's dressed for comfort, but my cock doesn't understand the difference between when she dresses for him or for the world; my cock always thinks she dresses just for him.

And there is no hiding my reaction to seeing her stomach in the glass shower. She can see exactly what I think of her outfit.

She smiles, raising an eyebrow when she spots my growing erection.

"What do you want, Siren?" I ask, exhausted. *How can she already exhaust me and it's only seven in the morning?* I got a good night's sleep, I shouldn't be tired, but I am. Siren demands everything from me.

"Just to tell you to stop touching yourself and get ready. We have twenty minutes before our plane leaves."

"I'm not touching myself."

"Maybe you should if you aren't going to be able to control yourself with that *thing* all day," she says with a smirk.

I stiffen in annoyance. "You seemed to like my cock just fine last night."

"Twenty-minutes, plane, St. John," she says and then darts out.

I sigh. It seems that all of my planning doesn't matter. We are taking a plane, not a boat. And I don't have the energy to fight with her. I'm surprised she's willing to help me. I thought she might enjoy seeing me struggle with a task she does on a daily basis. But I remember she wants these stupid games with Julian over as much as I do. The faster they're completed, the faster she can return to her life before me.

I finish showering and get dressed. I quickly throw some extra clothes in a bag and pack up my gun and bullets. If we are flying commercial, I'll have to leave them in my truck, but I'd rather have them if at all possible, which is why I'd rather take the boat. I'm sure Siren knows where to buy weapons once we arrive.

"God, you're such a diva. Thirty minutes in the only bathroom in this house is excessive. I had to do my hair and makeup without a mirror," Siren gripes from the hallway, but there is a smile in her eyes. She's happy. And I'd like to think the sex last night had something to do with it.

"Just enjoying my last few minutes away from you."

She pats my arm like I'm a child, but the second her hand touches mine, the sparks have returned. She jumps back suddenly, not expecting the connection to still be there. We both hoped that after we fucked, the constant throbbing for each other would stop. But nope—if anything, it just got worse.

I clear my throat. "Did you pack a bag?"

She shakes her head.

"Do you want to?"

"Nope, we should be able to get this done in a night, two, tops. I'll buy whatever clothes and things I need when we get there."

My eyes widen. I'm not used to traveling with a woman who is so low-maintenance. But that's Siren. The most demanding, needy woman one minute and easy-going and independent the next.

"Let's go then," I say, throwing my overnight bag over my shoulder and starting to walk to my truck.

Siren follows, jumping into the passenger seat. She flicks the radio on, apparently not okay with any silence. I'm not a talker as it is, and I'm especially not a talker at seven in the morning when I haven't had coffee. More quiet still after I made a huge mistake in fucking Siren last night.

It was great, a night I will never forget. But now, anytime I'm around her, my cock gets rock hard like he expects a repeat. *Not going to happen, bro.* But my self-talk does nothing to talk him down.

I start driving down the gravel road, hoping I'll be able to think about something else to make my jeans a little less tight, but Siren starts singing along to a Beyonce song, and I'm lost.

Her voice is intoxicating and alluring. It could convince any man into jumping over a cliff after hearing it. It's not just that her voice is beautiful; it's haunting and magical. It's different than any other voice I've heard. It's not flawless; she doesn't hit every note perfectly like Beyonce does on the radio; she changes her voice to fit her mood and her feelings. I don't even think she realizes that she's singing, that her voice isn't perfectly in tune with the melody, or that she's now changed several of the lyrics to suit her. When she sings, it's because she loves to sing. And there is nothing more captivating than that.

"Zeke! Watch out!" Siren screams all of a sudden.

I realize I've been watching her instead of paying attention to the road. I slam on the brakes just short of the edge of a cliff with only palm trees to break our fall.

"Shit," I curse under my breath. I realize the truck is most likely stuck in the sand on the side of the road.

We both breathe heavily.

"I think I should drive from now on; I'm tired of almost dying any time I get in the car with you. Or really, any time I'm around you," Siren says with a tiny smile, trying to lighten the tension.

"Know anything about how to get a truck unstuck in the sand?" I ask.

She laughs. "Even if I did, you're the one who got us into this predicament; you get us out. I'm not a mechanic or car person, though, no. My skills stop at being able to fire a gun, a little Krav Maga, and using my body to seduce men."

My heart clenches. She just had to mention seducing other men. *How many men have fallen for her? How many men have slept in her bed?* I'm just one of many. Last night meant nothing to her. I'm sure she's had her fill of men worshipping at her feet.

"Good, I plan on using your seduction skills to get to this Beckett guy," I say, leaning in close to her so she can feel my angry breath as I say it.

She frowns. "Sure."

My eyes flicker between hers. She's pissed. And turned on from the pink flush of her cheeks. *Maybe I have more of an effect on her than I think? Maybe she doesn't fuck men every night?* She was awfully tight for a woman who I assume has fucked every man she's ruined.

Stop thinking about sex.

Ugh.

I jump out of the car, and confirm our predicament—we are stuck in the sand. I find a piece of driftwood to stick under the wheel to give the truck some traction. And then I signal for Siren to step on the gas. She's already moved over to the driver's seat, and I know she won't let me drive anymore. Although, I wouldn't get us into such predicaments if she wouldn't distract me with her singing. Or her body. Or her presence, sitting next to me.

God, I'm so screwed.

She pulls back onto the road, and I jump in the passenger side—I'm a little sandier than when I jumped out, but otherwise, I'm good. She takes off toward the airport, turning the radio up in excitement at the next song.

I flick it off immediately.

"Why'd you do that?"

"Because your voice is what caused me to lose my dignity in the first place."

"Damn right, I won't let you drive when you almost got us killed, again." But she's smiling. She likes that I'm not arguing with her about me needing to drive my own truck.

Honestly, I prefer the passenger seat. It gives me more time to study her body without worrying about killing us. But her singing takes things too far. I'll jump her if she starts singing again. And then she'd be the one to crash us.

So instead, we ride in silence—something I'm used to and thrive in, giving me time to think clearly. Siren, on the other hand, seems irritable as we pull onto the airport's main road. I assume it's because she's still mad about the almost cliff dive we had, or maybe it's because she hasn't had her morning coffee yet either.

She doesn't talk to me yet as we head toward the private side of the airport. *Good, we aren't flying commercial, so I can bring my gun.*

"I'm going to talk to the pilot. We should be ready to leave in five minutes," Siren says after we enter the small terminal.

I nod and watch her walk away. I decide I should do something nice and get us both coffees for the flight. It's the right thing to do after fucking her last night. If I was being myself, I would have made her breakfast in bed, offered her a long soak in the tub, pampered her all morning, and then sent her flowers after she left. But this isn't a normal situation. We aren't dating. She hates my guts.

So I'll just settle on coffee.

While I'm standing in line for coffee, I notice a small stand with flowers. Flowers can't hurt either. Might get her to stop scowling at me all the time and like me enough for us to work together in peace. And honestly, I like being the nice guy everyone likes.

I buy two coffees and decide on a single red rose.

I walk in the direction I last saw Siren and find her standing next to a cute black woman. Siren is wearing her familiar scowl that only deepens the closer I get.

"Coffee black, like you like it," I say, holding out the coffee. And then I lean in so only she can hear. "And a flower because you saved my life back there."

She frowns and picks up a coffee from the table behind her. "I can get my own." She turns and starts walking out toward the tarmac.

I sigh, now I'm holding two coffees and a flower like an idiot.

The woman she was talking to smiles brightly.

"I'm Nora," she says.

"Zeke," I say.

"I like coffee and flowers."

"Oh, here, sure." I hand her the coffee and flower. She

tucks the flower behind her ear, just like I imagined Siren doing and then sips the coffee.

"Aria will come around. She's not the romantic type, if you know what I mean."

"A coffee and flower is romantic?"

"To most women, yes." Nora looks toward where Siren is already climbing up the stairs of a small propeller plane. "She's used to being independent and having to take care of herself. Don't take it personally."

"I don't. We aren't together."

"I know. But you should be," she says with a playful smile before heading toward the plane herself.

I jog after her. "Why do you say that? We're enemies stuck working together. Don't put ideas in Siren's head."

She stops. "Siren?"

"I mean, Aria."

This only makes her eyes brighten more, like she can understand our entire relationship from just one conversation.

"Well, I can't put any ideas into Siren's head. It's not possible. I've known the woman for years, and she does what she wants when she wants. But then you know that already."

"I do."

"I think you are just the kind of man she needs."

"And what kind of man is that?"

She sips her coffee, still smiling brightly in the way I wish Siren would every time she looks at me. "You seem like a smart man; you'll figure it out."

"You coming with us to St. John?"

"Better than that. I'm the one flying you."

I look her up and down. She's wearing jeans and a T-shirt. This woman is tiny. Can't be bigger than five foot two.

She's not dressed like any pilot I've ever seen, but I would trust this woman with my life and children.

"Lead the way then," I say, carrying my bag and coffee as I follow Nora up the stairs to the plane.

I don't spot Siren anywhere in the back of the plane. I even check the bathroom.

"Need anything before takeoff?" Nora asks, nodding toward the front where I see Siren sitting in one of the pilot seats.

I follow Nora up as she takes her seat and starts going through her checks.

"You a pilot now, too?" I ask Siren.

"Nope, just thought I'd keep my best friend company."

Best friend, huh? Finally, I've learned a fact about Siren.

"I think your best friend would prefer you ride in the back with me. That way, we can make a plan while your best friend focuses on flying the plane."

Siren looks from me to Nora, and I can tell they exchange a silent conversation. Nora may be on my side, but as she said earlier, no one persuades Siren to do anything unless she wants to.

Which is why her relationship with Julian is so weird. The only reason I can think of that Siren does as Julian says is because she wants to. Which means I have no hope of changing her mind.

"My friend would prefer if I keep her company," Siren says.

Nora gives me a look as if to say, *I'm sorry, I tried.*

I sigh and relent myself to sitting in the back of the plane, alone.

"So, who's the guy?" Nora asks with knowing eyes as she starts up the plane's engines.

"He's just a guy who works for Julian," I answer, keeping to the truth, mostly. Zeke does work for Julian, so it's not a lie, he's just not working for him by choice. But what Nora doesn't know won't kill her.

She sighs. "Ugh, I thought he was one of the good guys, but if he's working for Julian, there must be something wrong with him."

I take a sip of the coffee I got for myself. "Plenty."

"What? He's rude? Heartless? A bully? Sexist? Racist? An asshole?"

Nope, he's none of those things.

"Have a small dick?"

I shoot her a look.

She grins proudly. "Fine, what's wrong with him then?"

"He's insufferable, thinks he's better than everyone else, arrogant, noble, loyal—"

"Those all seem like positives to me," Nora frowns.

"Trust me, they're not." *Except sometimes that protective*

streak in him is mighty sexy. As is his loyalty and nobility. I even enjoy his arrogance.

We are silent as we take off. I glance over at her, waiting for more questions, and I notice her fidgeting with the flower Zeke bought for me but gave to her.

I grind my teeth together at the sight. *Why does he have to also be so fucking sweet?* We are enemies, and he bought me a damn coffee and flower. *Why?* Because he's a nice guy, that's why. When he dates women, he probably takes them on real dates, holds doors open, and sends them daily chocolates or flowers.

I'm not that type of woman—the type who wants him to be all romantic and cheesy. Even if we were dating, I don't want flowers. I don't want a man to buy me shit. *I just want...*

"Have you fucked him yet? Or is that why there is so much pent up frustration in this plane right now?" Nora asks. The way she wiggles her eyebrows and takes the flower from her ear and strokes my arm with it, I know she isn't into Zeke. But she thinks I am.

She's my best friend in the whole world. We met when I first came to the island at eighteen. She knows me better than anyone else. She's a rich princess who flies planes for fun, to have something to do, and to have the ability to travel at a moment's notice without having to coordinate with anyone else. She knows I will only ever tell her the truth. She knows my problem with being able to lie—I can't lie. So she waits for me to answer.

I sigh, I should have stayed in the back with Zeke. I may not be able to lie, but I can evade. "I'm going to check on Zeke."

She smirks triumphantly. I know she wanted me to go sit with him the whole time, but I really don't want to be anywhere near him. Not when I know there will be no more fucking. This trip might even be the last time we are alone together. For all I know, the rest of Julian's sins will be completed with someone else watching guard over him. We need to get back to a business relationship and stop undressing each other with our eyes.

But the sight in front of me when I step into the back of a plane makes me drool with need.

Zeke is sitting in his chair, his biceps and shoulders overflowing into the seat next to him. Good thing we are the only ones on this plane. If he had to sit next to someone, I'm not sure there would be room. Unless it was a woman, then she'd be more than happy to sit on his lap.

The heated look in his eyes when he spots me tells me exactly what's on his mind, but the way he's gripping the seat tells me he's nervous as hell about my friend's flying.

Nora makes a hard turn, and as I'm slung against the doorway, I remember my first time flying with her. She's more than capable of flying perfectly. She passed all her exams to fly a commercial flight with ease. But she prefers to live on the dangerous side of life and enjoys making her passengers push the limits too.

"Nervous flyer?" I ask, enjoying getting to tease Zeke.

"Not usually, but your friend has a death wish. I'm surprised you haven't taken over; her flying is far worse than my driving."

I fold my arms over my chest as I eat up the sight in front of me. "First, it's not possible to be worse at flying than you are at driving. Second, I would if I knew how to fly."

He scoffs. "Like you don't know how to fly."

I frown. "I don't. I don't know how to do everything."

"You sure act like it."

I'm just about to tell him off and go back to sitting up

front with Nora when the plane dips, and I stumble forward —right onto Zeke's lap.

His hands go to my hips, steadying me in his lap, as his eyes go to my face inspecting me for any sign of injury.

"Stop saving me," I whisper, out of breath and needy.

"Stop needing saving," he breathes back.

Another turn of the plane and my lips fall forward, so fucking close to his. His lips are beyond tempting for me to kiss. I want them. On my mouth. Sucking on my nipples. Tantalizing my pussy. Instead, his lips are parted, waiting for me to make the final move.

And the space between us is enough to remind me why I can't kiss him. Why fucking him was a one-time thing. Never again. *Never, never, never.*

My heart already hurts after one night. A second would leave me ruined.

I glare up front at Nora, who is purposefully flying like a maniac to ensure I landed in Zeke's lap. *Damn Nora and her matchmaking.*

"Ever joined the mile-high club?" Zeke asks, with desperation in his voice. He's not just asking me if I have, but if I want to.

"Been a member since 2015."

He frowns, the moment over as soon as I speak.

"Who? How? When?" he asks, perturbed to hear stories of me with another man.

But the angry expression on his face tells me everything he's thinking. He thinks I'm a whore. That because of my job, I sleep with any man who I or Julian want something from. That's not how this works. That's not who I am. Sure, I like sex, and I don't mind using it to get what I want on occasion. But I don't like Zeke thinking so little of me.

"We should be landing in about thirty minutes," I answer.

"It's just sex, Siren." He strokes my cheek.

"No, sex is never *just* sex. There is always something more. Sometimes romance, sometimes love, sometimes money, sometimes secrets. But there is always *something*."

"There is nothing more between us. Just two people who hate each other, are mortal enemies, and who happen to enjoy having sex with each other. With us, there are no emotions."

"I thought last night was a one-time thing."

"I've changed my mind."

My eyes flick to the front where Nora sits with a cup of coffee and flower meant for me. I turn back. "Flowers and coffee scream romance, Zeke."

He smirks. "I'm a nice guy, Siren. I'm not going to change who I am just because it makes you uncomfortable."

"I'm not going to change who I am, either."

And that's the problem. We need to change who we are to be together. As lovers. As friends. As *more*.

Neither of us will. Neither of us can.

"Truth or sin," Zeke starts, getting desperate. It's not even been twenty-four hours, and he's already begging for sex. Already wanting more.

My body warms, my body is hungry for his. I understand why he's doing this. It's taking all of my self-control not to kiss him and rip his clothes off right now.

"Zeke, we can't..."

"Can't or won't? You're a strong independent woman. You make your own decisions. You don't let me, or any other man, make your choices for you. What do you want?"

You.

In any capacity I can get you, for as long as I can get you.

My lover. My friend. My boyfriend.

But it's not fair. To either of us. We got our moment together. *Never again.*

He must read my decision in my eyes.

"Fine, then what's the harm in playing our game?"

"When I refuse to answer, you'll get what you want."

"I'll add a new rule then. I can't repeat a sin. Which means I can't fuck you again as my sin."

Hearing Zeke say he can't fuck me again hurts when every nerve in my body is shouting for him to do just that. *Would fucking him one more time really be the worst thing?*

"And I promise, no matter what, to never bring you coffee or flowers again. Nothing remotely considered romantic, regardless of what you decide."

"Good," I say. I hate the romantic stuff, and I hate being taken care of.

"Truth or sin? What vow did you promise Julian?" Zeke dips me back so he can look me dead in the eyes as I answer. Even if I was capable of lying, my body screams my honest secrets to him daily. *It's not my fault he doesn't realize the truth.*

"Sin." I bite my lip, waiting for him to do his best to tempt me. Kiss me, torment my breasts, undress me.

Instead, his eyes turn dark before he sits me back up and looks up to Nora.

"Hey, Nora," he shouts.

My mouth falls open. *What is he doing?*

"Yes, handsome?" Nora answers.

"What are you doing tonight? Want to grab dinner with me?" he asks.

I can practically feel Nora's eyes on me, trying to decide if she'll piss me off by going.

"Only if you take me to a steakhouse," she flirts back.

"Deal," Zeke shouts.

I hate him. He fucked me last night. Made it clear that he wanted to fuck me now. And then asked my best friend out right in front of me.

Fuck him.

And I want to. *Literally.*

Damn, why am I more attracted to this asshole version of Zeke instead of the gentleman version? What's wrong with me?

"Your turn," he says, daring me to say something to stop their date.

"Do you want to fuck Nora?" I ask, the question slipping out before I think.

Zeke raises an eyebrow as if he can't believe I just asked that question. And then his hand slides down my bare arm, then over my hip, teasing my skin and making chills run up and down my body. His hands tell me what his words won't—he doesn't want to sleep with Nora, he wants to fuck me.

"Yes," he breathes against my neck, sending the worst kind of chills through my body. They feel delicious, like I'm the only woman he could ever crave, while simultaneously feeling like death to my heart when he says he wants to fuck Nora.

Zeke may be able to tell a lie, but he won't during the game. It's our one rule he will never break. Because if I catch him in a lie, then I get to kill him. *Or maybe he thinks even if I can kill him, I never will?*

I'm so ridiculous thinking that he would lie to me just to get back at me when he knows the consequence of lying is death.

My teeth grind together so hard, I'm surprised my jaw hasn't broken yet. *I hate him. I hate him. I hate him,* I whine to myself.

I'm not the type of woman to complain. I'm the type of woman who goes after what she wants. And right now, I want Zeke to fuck me. To want me. Not Nora. Not any other woman.

Jesus, when did I get this jealous? Just let it go. I gave him up; he moved on. He was never mine anyway. *But damn, why did he have to move on with my best friend hours after he fucked me?*

Because that's not who Zeke is. He's loyal. He's sweet. He's kind. *So is he really falling for Nora in a matter of minutes, or I'm missing something?*

I'm not going to sit around waiting to see what the hell I'm missing. I'm going to kiss him. Fuck him. Remind him why he wants me and pull any secret he's not sharing out of his body.

I put my hand on Zeke's chest, intent on grabbing his shirt and pulling him to me roughly for a kiss to end all future kisses for him. I thought last night was incredible. I thought it easily topped all other nights. *But what if Zeke didn't feel that way?*

Just as my fingers curl around the fabric of his shirt, Nora hollers, "We're about to hit some turbulence. Buckle up back there; we land in five."

Zeke cocks his head in a challenging way. My chance has passed. I got my one night with Zeke; now it's over.

I climb off his lap and into the chair next to him, next to the window, and buckle my seatbelt. But it's impossible to escape him. His shoulder and thigh rub up against me. My stomach tightens, my pussy aches remembering how he felt inside me last night—something I gave up, all to guard my heart and his.

I know it's for the best. If it hurts now, I can't imagine how it would feel to fuck him a dozen times and still have to let him go. Still, when faced with the fact that Zeke will end up in Nora's bed tonight, it all feels like a giant mistake.

16

———

ZEKE

*W*HAT AM *I* DOING?

Playing with fire, that's what.

Everything changed on that death trap of a plane. While I was fearing for my life, I realized what I want—Siren.

Whatever I can get from her—sex, friendship, love. Even just the snarky conversation. I want her. All of her ideally, but I'll take what I can get.

I know our time together is limited. That this thing between us isn't going to last forever. But I have a new mission.

And my mission is to fuck Siren in every position and place imaginable. Fuck her until she either falls for me or until I finish my sins for Julian. And keep myself from falling for Siren in the process.

Easy—I hate her. But there is a fine line between love and hate. One that I've never crossed before, and won't with Siren. I could never fall for a woman so heartless.

We decide to setup a base of operations at a local hotel first. Siren gives me a dirty look as she checks us into our rooms. I let her book my room too even though I'm guessing she's going to find the only room with a twin bed to try and keep me from fucking Nora, who I'm sure is staying in the same room as Siren.

Siren hands me a keycard. "Sorry, they only had one king bed left. So Nora and I took it since we are sharing. Gave you a twin bed."

I snatch the keycard from her hand with a grin. "As long as I don't have to listen to you snore all night, I'm good."

She pouts. It's adorable, so I smile. If Nora weren't standing next to her with an even bigger grin on her face, Siren would let me have it. Instead, she turns and stomps off.

"You're really getting under her skin," Nora says with a wink before following her friend toward the elevator banks.

"I'll stop by your room at eight to take you to dinner," I shout after Nora, loudly enough so Siren can easily hear. Siren just pushes the elevator button a hundred times, like that will make the elevator arrive any faster.

"Great, it will give me time to go shopping for the perfect dress," Nora responds with a wink, knowing exactly what she's doing—driving Siren mad, so she'll fling herself back into my arms.

I start walking toward the elevators as one opens, and Siren and Nora step on. But Siren presses the button for the doors to close just as I reach them. I could stick my arm between the gap to keep them from closing, but I decide not to.

But there is no denying the heat in her eyes and the want in her belly, as her lips part like she's dying for water, when really she's dying to taste me.

I make it up to my hotel room a few minutes later. My room includes two twin beds that would be perfect for Siren and Nora to use, but I won't complain. I have no intention of fucking Nora tonight, even if that's what I told Siren during our game.

It wasn't a lie, per se. I'm a man after all, and men like sex with hot women. Nora is attractive; I'd love to fuck her. But nowhere near as much as I'd love to fuck Siren. If given the choice, I'd always choose Siren. But it was fun to tease Siren and know I'm driving her mad all night. Almost as mad as when I do nice things for her like bring her coffee.

I don't know what I want more—to be nice to her and watch her squirm, or flirt with another woman and get her evil eye and snarky mouth. It's a win-win for me. Although, I know which version of Siren is at the top of my list. The one naked on my bed, willing to let me do anything to her body.

I grab my laptop out of my bag, knowing I can't spend the day thinking about Siren. I have a job to do—hunt down Eli Beckett and kill him after getting every piece of information I can from him.

Nora is just part of my plan. It's easier to get to a man like Beckett with a hot woman on my arm. If he thinks we're random newlyweds on our honeymoon, as opposed to the assassins we are, he will let his guard down. And if he doesn't buy that, then I can use her to distract him.

A quick search of all the bars and clubs in the area gives me a very good idea where a man in the underground would most likely conduct business. I recognize several of the clubs from my time with Enzo.

I toss my laptop onto the bed, planning on spending the rest of the day meeting with anyone who might know Eli Beckett. I just have to be careful no one who knows me notices me and reports back to Enzo that I'm alive. He's better off thinking I'm dead.

———

I knock on the hotel bedroom door at five till eight; showing up early to a date shows how excited I am. Showing up with a large bouquet of expensive flowers is romantic. Showing up early with expensive flowers, chocolates, and champagne is probably overdoing it. But I don't ever get to go out on dates. And I know the sappier I am to Nora, the more I will drive Siren insane.

I attached a sappy love note to each item I brought. I really hope after we leave, and Siren is left alone in the hotel room, that Siren will read every note and realize I wrote each one for her. If she would just tell me her truth, I would save her.

If she opened her heart, I would claim it.

And if she decided to only open her legs for me again, and not her heart, then I'd give her the best sex of her life.

The door opens, and Nora steps out in a smoking hot red dress that brings out the highlights in her black hair. She's left her hair natural in a pile of springy curls on top of her head, and the dress hugs her petite curves, clinging to her black skin.

Beautiful.

But not mine.

I don't get any ache to kiss her. I don't get an animalistic desire to push her against the wall and devour her. I don't feel anything other than respect for her beauty. I'd settle for her any night, but not when I know Siren is the other option.

"These are for you," I say, holding out the items to her.

"Wow, Zeke, these are beautiful. And oh my god! Dom! I haven't had that in forever. We will have to drink this when we get back tonight."

I step into their suite and put the bouquet of flowers in

the small kitchenette area, while she puts the Dom in the fridge.

And then I spot her—the only woman my heart bleeds for.

She's flicking through her phone wearing sweatpants and my T-shirt, completely ignoring me, and somehow she's still the most appealing thing in the room. I love that she is still wearing my T-shirt. I never want her to take my T-shirt off again. *That is unless she's undressing for me.*

"Have any plans tonight, Siren?" I ask.

She ignores me.

"I love that nickname for you, Aria, how did you come up with it? I know there's a story I'm missing?" Nora asks.

"There is. Siren here saved me. Pulled me from the sea like she was a mermaid, and I was a drowning sailor."

"Like *The Little Mermaid*," Nora squeals, liking this story a lot.

"Exactly like *The Little Mermaid*," I say, even though I've never seen the movie. I see Siren tense because clearly, she understands the reference. "But unlike the fairytale, Siren here wasn't actually saving me. She was using me so she could serve me to her boss. Hence the name Siren. She lures men to their deaths. And I was one of the stupid men who fell for her games."

Siren frowns but doesn't look up from her phone. I swear it looks like my words wounded her, though. And I hate it. I hate hurting her.

This was a mistake. I can't flirt with Nora; it will hurt Siren too much.

But then, Siren snaps her head in my direction. Whatever hurt was there a moment ago is gone now. "Don't act like you are some prince I hurt. You aren't the prince in this story, Zeke. You are just the damn errand boy, the guy who sacrifices himself for the prince he serves. Someday, I'll find my prince, but he sure as hell isn't you." And with that, she gets up and slams the bedroom door in my face.

My stomach twists, I'm not even going to be able to enjoy dinner knowing that Siren is hurting this badly. Nora, on the other hand, seems extremely happy. She claps her hands together in excitement.

"What are you doing?" I ask.

"Cheering you two on. I wish I had a video camera right now to tape you. This is good stuff, and I know I'm only getting half the story."

"I thought you were her friend. Why are you happy she's in pain?"

Nora takes my arm. "Best friend. And I'm happy because it means she actually feels something for a man. She wouldn't act jealous or vengeful if she didn't like you."

"Maybe I should talk to her instead of going?"

"No, we are going to enjoy a dinner. Trust me, by the time we get back, Siren will be throwing herself at you, and you'll be spending your night in this bed while I sleep in the twin bed downstairs."

"That or she'll have her gun out to shoot me," I mumble under my breath.

Nora giggles. "You know her well. You'll either get the best sex of your life, or you'll end up shot."

I nod.

"Would getting shot be worth it?" she asks, not hiding the hope in her voice.

"Yes, I've already gotten shot by the woman. And trust me, it was worth it."

Nora is giddy with excitement. But it's only because she doesn't know the rest. She doesn't know Siren betrayed me. She doesn't know my only goal is to kill Siren's boss, and maybe even Siren if I can't get her to promise not to go after my friends. My only goal is to get back to my family—Enzo, Kai, Langston, Liesel...

Nora studies me closely. "You're going to break my friend's heart, aren't you?"

I chuckle. "Your friend doesn't have a heart to break."

And then Nora slaps me.

"What was that for?"

She frowns. "For when you inevitably break her. I just hope you are one of the good guys who's able to pick the pieces back up after the damage is done."

I sigh, I don't know what I'm getting myself into. These women are going to kill me. If Nora doesn't kill me on this date, Siren will when we get back.

We go to dinner, have a nice meal, and hop around a few bars looking for Beckett. And when we show up at the third bar, it turns out I won't have to wait until the end of the night to see Siren again after all.

17

SIREN

ZEKE and his perfect date with Nora.

Fuck them and their nice steak dinner.

Fuck Zeke in his suit pants and jacket. *Who does he think he's fooling anyway?* He looks ridiculous in that suit, with this hair pulled up in a man bun, and his clean-shaven look. His smooth, sculpted jawline I want to rub my face all over.

Screw him. I don't care that he dressed up for Nora, when I've never seen him in anything other than jeans and a T-shirt. *Nora can have him.*

And fuck his flowers, his chocolates, his champagne. *Who does he think he's impressing with that shit?*

Nobody. That's who. Definitely not me.

But then I had to be an idiot after Zeke and Nora left on their 'date.' I read the damn notes attached to each gift. I expected them to be impersonal and stupid. Something like:

To: Nora

Enjoy these flowers. I'm excited about our date.

—Zeke

. . .

But that's not what any of the notes said. I grabbed the note attached to the flowers first. Flowers I'm sure will give me allergies. *That's just what I need—a stuffy nose to deal with the rest of the trip.*

To the woman who is beauty and strength itself. These flowers are both to honor and prove that I have hope for *more.*

What the hell does that mean? More?

I snatched the second note, the one attached to the champagne next.

To the woman who is as unpredictable, explosive, and sexy as this champagne, I can't wait to watch you explode *again.*

Fuck, these notes aren't meant for Nora. They are for me. Zeke knew I'd snoop as soon as they left. *Damn him. I'm not reading the last note. I'm not...*But of course, I did.

To the woman who tasted more delicious than these chocolates. These are to remind you how incredible we were in bed together and how I can't wait to do it *again.*

I popped one of the chocolates in my mouth—annoyed,

angry, and needy. *Does he really think these gifts are supposed to change my mind?* I'm not fucking him, and I sure as hell am not giving him a chance at *more* or doing anything *again*. These notes were so damn cheesy and romantic—not the way to win my heart or a second night together.

But then I saw another note sticking out of one of the chocolates.

Don't do it.

I snagged it and read it.

I know you think these are all cheesy and not remotely romantic. Don't worry, they aren't for you, snoopy. They are for Nora.

—Zeke

P.S. Don't eat the chocolate or drink the champagne. They are for Nora, my date, who is not you.

I dropped the second piece of chocolate I was about to eat.

No, he doesn't control me.

I grabbed two and popped them in my mouth.

After that, I knew I wasn't sitting in the hotel room all night waiting for them to get back from their date. Nora asked me if I liked him. I didn't answer, which was my way of avoiding lying to her. But she knows the truth anyway.

Yes, I like him.

No, I don't plan on breaking any more hearts—mine, especially.

So she went on the date. And she won't fuck him. But if I know Nora, she'll do some torturing of her own. Serves Zeke right for trying to make me jealous.

That leads me here to a bar, sipping a martini while I wait for them to realize Beckett is here. It's almost eleven, I expected them sooner. I know Zeke didn't just bring Nora on this date to taunt me. He also brought her because he knows the best way to get to Beckett is through a woman. But I thought Zeke's skills were better than this. That or he is really enjoying his date.

Beckett's been sitting at this bar for the past hour, sipping a bourbon on ice. While I've been trying to keep my distance, keep him from noticing me, so that when Zeke and Nora do show up, I can make my move.

Finally, at a quarter past eleven, they show up. Zeke spots me instantly, but it's not surprising since I immediately spot them too.

Nora is giggling at something he said. It's not a fake laugh, and it puts me on edge because Zeke seldom makes a joke. *But he did for her.*

No matter how attentive Zeke is to Nora, there is no denying that my connection to Zeke is stronger. He can't not notice me, just as I can't not notice him as he walks into the room. I just feel him, deep to my bones, like his presence is sending out alarm bells directed only at me. And I still can't figure out why it happens. Other than it's biological. Science says we should be together even if my brain knows better. Zeke is the kind of man I avoid.

No, I avoid all men. Men destroy my life.

Zeke moves his hand down Nora's back, and he guides her over to where I'm sitting at the end of the bar.

"What are you doing here?" Zeke asks.

"I thought I'd help you out locating Beckett and taking

him down. That way, you wouldn't have to stop your date," I answer.

Zeke scowls. "Beckett's here?"

"Yep, at your five o'clock. The man in flannel and missing his right arm."

"Flannel? Really? On an island like this? He must run really cold," Nora asks, surprised.

Or he's not from around here, which is why Julian wants him dead before he takes over any more of Julian's business.

Zeke doesn't seem at all surprised by any of the information I just told him about the man. Which means he's done his research and found out everything I have.

"So, what's your plan?" Zeke sighs.

"What makes you think I have a plan? This is your mission. I'm just here to babysit and make sure you don't hurt my best friend in the process."

Nora smiles at me.

"Because you have a plan. And as you said, I don't want to hurt Nora. You've been watching him all night. How do you think we should play it?"

I grin. *I win.* Although, when Zeke tightens his grip around Nora's waist, I feel like I lost—big time.

"I go flirt with him and get him somewhere alone. I better move quickly because there is a bachelorette party with their eyes on him," I say.

"But—" Zeke starts.

I don't let him finish, but I can hear the pain in his voice. And I glance back for a second and see the flash of worry in his eyes.

Don't fuck him, he mouths to me.

I glare back. *Really? He's going to try and give me orders?* And orders to not fuck him. *Does he really think I'd do that?*

Fuck a horrible man like Beckett, who is about to die by Zeke's hands? Not likely.

But then Zeke thinks I just whore my body out to anyone. It almost makes me want to fuck the guy. Beckett is good looking after all, if you are into flannel.

I decide to play on his gentlemanly charms. I stumble up to the bar, almost falling in my stiletto heels I'm quite adept in walking in.

And right on cue, Beckett catches me.

I feel Zeke's eyes on me, and I give him a wink as I play the damsel in distress role that worked so well on Zeke.

"Are you okay, ma'am?" Beckett asks.

Ugh, ma'am. "Oh, excuse me. It's just a bit slippery there," I say, slurring my words just enough to sound tipsy, not drunk.

He smiles back. "Let me order you a drink. What are you having?"

"Martini," I say, even though I hate the drink. On nights like this, I drink it because it's sexy and sophisticated, and the olive that comes with it is great for flirting.

Beckett flags the bartender down and orders me a martini and him another bourbon. *This was easy, too easy.*

My suspicions are up, but when Beckett checks out my cleavage that I may have bronzed and used makeup to make extra voluptuous tonight, I know I'm just having an exceptionally good night.

"You here alone?" he asks, looking behind me.

He saw me here with Zeke and Nora. *Observant man. He must be good at what he does.*

"No, but then you already know that," I say, keeping eye contact with him as I sip my drink. I consider touching his arm to see if we get that little zing that sometimes happens with Zeke, but it feels like too much too fast. And I don't want him to get suspicious.

"I did. Do your friends want to join us?" he asks.

"Do you want them to?"

"No," he says with a smile.

I push my breasts out as I take another drink. "I'm Aria."

"Beckett."

Interesting, he goes by his last name.

"And what do you do, Beckett?"

"I'm a cattle farmer."

I raise an eyebrow. His shirt does seem to scream that, so it's not a bad lie, but I know it's not the truth.

"And what do you do?"

I opened myself up for that question. I can seduce and lie with my body, but I can't with my words. I fucking can't. So I make my move. I grab the toothpick with the olive on the end and put the olive in my mouth. Sucking slowly and seductively on the olive as I pull the toothpick out.

His eyes are entranced on my lips. *I've got him.*

I go in for the closer. I brush my fingers over his arm.

"Right now...I want to *do* you."

His body tenses and heats at my words.

I smile. "Sorry, was that too forward of me."

He clears his throat. "No, not at all. I'd—"

But he doesn't finish that thought, because Zeke and Nora are standing behind me.

"Introduce us to your friend, Aria," Zeke says with a commanding voice. All I can focus on is the fact that he called me Aria.

I grit my teeth, forcing myself to continue smiling as I turn toward Zeke and Nora. Zeke has his arm thrown casually over Nora's shoulder, and he's lightly stroking her neck half-mindedly like he doesn't even realize he's doing it.

But Nora does, because she has a delirious look on her face, and her eyes close every other second as she makes small cooing sounds. That is, until her eyes open and she sees Beckett. Her eyes go wide as she realizes the man has lost an arm, but then they quickly turn soft when she takes in his tight body and bright smile.

I sigh. This is why I don't bring Nora with me when I meet dangerous men. She gets all googly-eyed and then gets mad when I kill them.

"Zeke, Nora, this is my friend Beckett. Beckett, these are my annoying friends who were just leaving, Zeke and Nora."

Zeke holds his left hand out, and Beckett shakes it. "Zeke, huh? I think I know a Zeke."

Zeke frowns, obviously not recognizing this man, but annoyed that Beckett seems to recognize him.

"I don't get out much, never been to St. John. You're probably remembering a different man," Zeke says.

Beckett nods slowly, and I'm not sure he's convinced. *Fuck, did Zeke just screw everything up by coming over here and getting recognized?*

"I'm Nora." She holds her left hand out to Beckett, who is smiling cautiously at the woman, like he's afraid she's going to bite him. Knowing Nora, she might.

I grin at the interaction. Nora seems to have distracted Beckett long enough for me to scowl at Zeke.

Really? Was this necessary? I had him.

He raises a scowling eyebrow. *Yea, you had him about to jump into your bed.*

So?

He stiffens and turns his attention back to Beckett. Conversation over.

I grab my drink, needing more alcohol, but when I lift

my drink to my lips, I realize that I already finished it when I thought I was going home with Beckett.

I raise my hand to flag down the bartender. I'm going to need a lot more alcohol and something stronger than a martini to get me through tonight.

The bartender smiles as he stops in front of me. "What can I get you, gorgeous?" He winks at me as he says it.

And in an instant, both Zeke and Beckett surround me, ready to defend my honor against the friendly bartender. Both men try to put their arms around my shoulder but only end up bumping arms awkwardly in the process.

"She'll have a martini," Beckett says at the same time Zeke says, "Another."

I lean forward, trying to escape both men. "Actually, your most expensive scotch, neat."

The bartender's eyes light up at that, like I'm telling him a secret the two bozos next to me don't know.

"I'll have that right up," the man says, not even bothering to ask if anyone else wants a drink.

But with the bartender gone, the tension is high. I give Nora a *please help me control Zeke* look, but she's still fawning all over Beckett, touching his arm, and batting her eyelashes. She may have enjoyed Zeke's attention before when she thought she was making me jealous and matchmaking Zeke and me, but now that there is an actual man in the picture who she could take home to her bed, she's changed course. I would support her completely, if I didn't think Beckett was a dangerous man who might drug, rape, or kill her.

Nora, I implore with my eyes to help me out by getting Zeke's attention. She doesn't. Instead, she keeps talking Beckett's head off.

I sigh—deciding I'll just have to wait until she's done talking to get Beckett's attention again.

"What are you doing? I was just about to close the deal," I hiss so that only Zeke can hear me.

He glares, his eyes burning into mine like he can't believe I found what I was about to do acceptable. "And I couldn't let you."

"I don't need you to protect my honor, Zeke. I'm a woman fully capable of making her own decisions. If I wanted to sleep with him, I would. If I didn't, I wouldn't."

"Well, I—"

Zeke is interrupted when the bartender returns and hands me my drink. "It's on the house," he says, winking at me.

That snaps both Zeke and Beckett's attention his way, earning a united scowl from both men.

"Thank you," I say sweetly, taking the drink and sipping on it, the liquid giving me life and enough energy to deal with both of these men. I make sure to brush my hand against the bartender's after I take my drink. If Zeke and Beckett weren't standing next to me, I'd be getting his number right now.

"So, Beckett, do you dance?" I ask, needing to get him away from Zeke and Nora.

He winces and looks down at his missing arm. "I wasn't very good before I lost my arm, and I'm not any better now."

"How did you lose your arm?" Nora asks, always the nosy one and not gentle in how she asks her questions.

"Car accident," Beckett says, taking a slow sip of his drink, his eyes on me. I can read through the lie. He didn't lose it in a car accident. He lost it doing something dangerous. Which is why I don't want him anywhere near my friend. And it's why I have to make sure he ends up dead.

I finish my drink in one large gulp, and I can feel both Zeke and Beckett's eyes on me as I swallow. I lean forward to grab Beckett's hand to pull him on the dance floor and not take no for an answer, but Zeke can apparently read my mind and knows my next move.

He grabs my arm before I have the chance, pulling me sharply toward the dance floor.

"Dance with me," he commands.

And then I'm in his strong arms, feeling like this is where I've belonged the whole time, and knowing I'm so fucking screwed.

18

———

ZEKE

I'VE NEVER FELT SO much rage in my entire life as I did watching Siren flirt with that man. It was so easy for her. Within seconds she had Beckett dopey-eyed, drooling, and ready to do whatever she asked of him. She is very good. *Too good.*

But then I knew that. She had me falling for her within a few seconds of meeting her, even with me delirious, drowning, and half-dead. I knew she was special. Every man who meets her knows that. It's why she has some deal with Julian. It's why she got me here, doing Julian's bidding. It's why Beckett almost walked right into her death trap.

I'm not special. Siren has treated me like every other man she's ever encountered. Like I'm a mark she's going after. And when she squeezes everything she can get from me, she'll get rid of me, just like she plans on doing with Beckett.

But with Siren in my arms, our bodies moving together on the dance floor, I forget about all of that. I may hate her, but she's hard not to fall for all the same.

"How do you do that?" I whisper into her hair, breathing

in everything that makes Siren, Siren. Her intoxicating smell that's a mix of sweet and spice, just like her.

"Do what?"

"Make me like you."

She gives me an *are you absurd* look.

I laugh. Maybe I am, because she's done nothing to make me fall for her. In fact, I'd say she's tried to get me to hate her.

"You are the one trying to get me to fall for you with your chocolates and flowers and stupid notes."

I grin. *She read the notes.*

I turn her toward me, smelling her breath.

"What are you doing?" she asks.

"Looking for evidence." Then I brush my thumb over her bottom lip. "Yep, right there. You had chocolate still on your lip. I told you I bought those for Nora, not you."

She frowns. "I don't have chocolate on my lip."

I suck my thumb that was just over her lip, watching her eyes dilate, wanting me to suck something of hers. "Not anymore, you don't."

She sighs, and it's part desperation, part exhaustion, part need.

"What are we doing, Zeke? We are supposed to be figuring out a way to get Beckett on his own, not pretending we like each other when we both just want more sex."

"Then, we should talk about the sex."

"No, we shouldn't."

I spin her and then pull her tight to my body. "Why not?"

She opens her mouth and then closes it quickly. She's seldom at a loss for words, and I'm not sure I like waiting for her witty comeback. "Because sex will complicate things."

I chuckle. "Not possible. We fucked, we still hate each

other. We are both still doing the job required of us. Sex did nothing but make our relationship more enjoyable."

"I just...can't."

Can't—I hate that word. Especially falling from her lips.

"I'm not giving up," I say.

And with a heavy smile, she says, "I never expected you to."

A challenge—I like a challenge. I just have no idea how to win when it comes to Siren.

By killing Julian and her.

But that's not the way I want to win. I want to win her over. I want her to want me in the same way I want her. I want her to fall for me like I stupidly fell for her.

And then what? I'll hurt her? I could never. But at least I would know I have the power too, just like she does. But unlike her, I won't rip out her heart and set it on fire just because I can. I would take care of her heart, even if I never loved her back.

The song turns slow, and I think Siren is going to use it as an excuse to stop dancing with me. She doesn't. She rests her head on my chest, and her arms go around my waist like she's hugging me, like she never wants to let me go.

I drape my arms over her shoulders, and we sway—slowly and carefully, like we are just dancing to the music, but we are dancing on each other's hearts. One wrong move could destroy us both.

I glance over at Beckett, who is listening to Nora ramble but is watching us.

I smirk. *She's mine, you asshole.*

I close my eyes and just live in the moment. This moment where Siren doesn't hate me and I don't want her dead. This moment where it doesn't matter that we are enemies or lovers or even friends. We are just together, dancing to a song neither of us will remember tomorrow. But this peaceful moment, we will remember forever.

The song stops too quickly. And I feel her dip out of my arms, mumbling something about having to go to the bathroom. I let her go because I'm stupid.

And when I glance back over where Beckett was sitting, he's gone. And so is Siren. Nora just gives me a shrug.

Fuck.

19

SIREN

IF MY LIFE WERE A SOUNDTRACK, it would be a shitty one. The kind that on first listen sounds great. The music is catchy, and there is just the right amount of emotional, slow songs to fill the track. But listening a second or third time makes you realize it's far too dramatic, has far too few happy endings, and the romance is just one sad depression into despair.

That's my life. From the outside, my life looks good. But once you dig in, you realize how complicated and shitty it really is.

Music is my life. Every important moment in my life had its own song to go with it—even if I was only playing the song in my head.

And dancing with Zeke to Never Give Up by Sia was the perfect song to describe how I feel. Dancing with a man who in another life would be the man I gave up everything for and never stopped fighting for. The man I would marry tomorrow because he's the rare good man in a sea of evil. But I don't live in a different life; I live in this life. I live in a bad soundtrack.

My life isn't Sia or Ariana Grande. My life is like a Taylor Swift love song, filled with regrets and unhappy endings.

"So you and Zeke?" Beckett asks as I walk with him out of the nightclub.

"Old flames. He's dating again, but I don't think he's fully moved on," I say, leaning into Beckett's chest as we walk to his car.

"And you? Have you moved on?" Beckett asks.

No, but then we haven't really had a chance to just 'be' in the first place.

"Do you really care if I've moved on? I'm going home with you," I say.

He smirks and then strokes my face. "By the end of the night, I'll make sure I'm the only man you think about."

I nod, but I doubt it. He could be the most amazing man in bed, and it wouldn't matter. Because I'm stupidly hung up on the oaf, who is still back at the bar about to take Nora back to his hotel room to fuck her as revenge for what he thinks I'm about to do.

I'm on the wrong side of Beckett to hold his hand, so he nudges me over until I'm on his left side and then takes my hand in his.

"Where'd you come from, Aria?"

"I'm a world traveler. But I love it here on the sand, on the beach, near the ocean. And you? Flannel? You obviously aren't from around here."

He smiles at that. "No, I'm from the arctic, the cold, the wilderness."

I tug on his beard. "I like the wilderness."

He leans his head to my side, closing our gap. "I like you."

I scrape my teeth over my bottom lip. "Yea? What do you like?"

I wait for the answer I always get when I ask a drunk man that question. You're beautiful, striking, sexy—something about my physical features.

"I like that you danced with an ex while flirting with me."

I stop walking. "You like that I'm a tease and a whore?"

He looks like I just slapped him. "No, I just meant you know your own value. You are more than just a pretty face. You aren't coming home with me because I'm your only option to get laid tonight. You weighed all of your options. I saw you sitting at the bar all night. You judged every man who walked in, deciding if he was worthy. Even worthy of just one night with you. You narrowed it down between me and your ex. And even then, you made it clear going home was also an option. You are an independent woman who doesn't need a man. I like that."

He puts his hand in his pocket, waiting for me to make the next move since I'm a strong, independent woman and all that. I like that he's letting me make the next move. But sometimes, I want a man I can depend on. A man who will take care of me. A man who does things for me in spite of the fact that I can do it for myself—make my own money, get myself off, and fight my own battles. Sometimes, I want a man to do all those things.

Beckett smiles, shaking his head at me.

"What?" I ask, knowing he can read me well. I still don't know what he does exactly, but he's skilled at reading people.

"You'll find that man someday; I'm just not him."

"How did you read my mind?"

He shrugs. "People are easy to read."

"Is that why you stick to herding cattle?"

He laughs. "Yes, cattle are way more interesting."

I grab the collar of his shirt and pull him to me. "I think you're interesting."

And then I kiss him, because I need to make the first move. If he tried to kiss me, I'd probably slap him or something. He's worried about that too, which is why he's been keeping his distance. But now that our lips are pressed together, he's not being so cautious.

His hand runs down my back over my ass, and then he squeezes as our lips press hard together, urgently. Our lips part and our tongues tangle in a familiar dance. It's a great fucking kiss. Beckett knows how to part his lips, move his tongue, dip his head to deepen the kiss. He knows how to use his one hand to press our bodies together and send little chills down my back. I even get little butterflies in my stomach when he kisses me because I know what happens next. It's exciting and new, but it's not Zeke.

Fuck, it's not Zeke.

I thought fucking him once was enough. But it's clear now that once wasn't enough to rid my feelings of him. I need to fuck Zeke until it's boring, no longer new. Until we've done all the usual positions. Until there is nothing new to explore with each other. Until we crave someone else.

Beckett ends the kiss. "My place or yours?"

"Yours," I say with a smile.

He wiggles his eyebrows behind him. Turns out, Beckett's hotel is right behind us.

I grin as he pulls on my hand, but I feel familiar chills run down my body. The intense kind that only comes from one man—Zeke.

I turn my head and see him walking down the sidewalk alone. He saw the kiss, and he looks like Godzilla about to destroy an entire village.

Maybe it's for the best. Zeke won't want me after he saw me kiss another man. And even though my body craves Zeke, no one will get hurt this way.

Beckett pulls me through the lobby's glass doors and then to the elevator bay. He's a gentleman, holding my hand as we wait for the elevator doors to open, but once inside, he's an animal.

He fists my ponytail as he pulls my head back to kiss me hard.

Focus on this kiss. Let the tingles I feel on my lips ignite a new fire—for any man other than Zeke.

Nothing. The tingles go nowhere. It's nice, but not holy-fucking-hot. It's just pleasant.

But when I look at Beckett, I know he's feeling a lot more than just nice. He's excited and happy about what comes next, and I play along with him.

We stumble back, groping each other, and stopping to kiss as we make our way to his hotel room. I take everything in as we walk. The escape route through the emergency stairs. The fire alarm. Then ten other rooms on this floor. The security camera in the corner. Even the stain two feet from Beckett's room I purposefully step over because, ew.

And once we are in Beckett's room, I realize one thing right away. He's messy as hell.

"Sorry about the mess," Beckett says.

"Ever hear of a hamper?" I ask against his lips, noticing all his clothes piled everywhere.

"Nope." He kisses back, already grabbing at my shirt, trying to pull it up.

I laugh when he yanks my shirt up, but it gets stuck around my ears, and we both have to slow down. Finally, he gets my shirt off, and his eyes devour my black lace bra and cleavage.

"Damn," he says.

I blush, biting my lip, liking the attention, even though I know how this night ends.

"Your turn," I say, grabbing his shirt and unbuttoning the flannel. I'm not sure what I expect when I undress him, but I wasn't expecting abs. *So many abs.*

"Impressive," I say, kissing the first ab. Zeke is big, thick, bulk muscle. While Beckett has thin, sleek muscles. The two men couldn't be more different.

I grab the hair tie holding my hair up in a sleek ponytail and let my hair down. He watches my hair fall with large eyes.

And then I push his bare chest, and he walks back until he hits the bed. He scoots up the bed, leaning back against the headboard while I climb up his body, putting one leg on each side of his, straddling him. His hand rests on my hip as I lean forward and kiss him, forcefully and deliciously. I kiss him to distract him, to make him forget with hopes that if I kiss him hard enough, I'll forget too. Not him, but Zeke.

But no amount of kissing can erase Zeke's kisses from my mind.

I reach into my back pocket, pull out a syringe, and then jab it into Beckett's neck.

"Sorry," I say as he slumps down. The drugs will knock him out for a bit until Zeke gets here and we can go through his stuff and decide what to do with him. I grab a shirt from the floor and tie his arm to the headboard. It won't hold him for long if he wakes up, but it will be one more obstacle to keep him from attacking us straight away.

I glance around the room that is going to take us hours to go through. There is way too much crap. I could start now, but I decide to help myself to Beckett's whiskey while I wait for Zeke.

But I don't have to wait long because a pound on the door tells me Zeke is here, and he isn't happy.

20

ZEKE

I SHOULD HAVE TURNED AROUND. I should have walked to my own hotel and forgot what I saw. Maybe drank my misery away? Or fucked Nora after all?

But I couldn't.

When I saw Siren kiss Beckett, my world ended. At first, I thought I was dreaming. It was all a nightmare. But soon I realized that it was real. I was standing on the sidewalk watching Siren kiss a man who is most likely the devil—a man who deserves to be killed, not fucked by an angel like Siren.

And in that moment, watching her kiss another man, I know that my life will forever be intertwined with hers. I will never be able to kiss another woman without thinking about Siren. I will never be able to watch a woman who looks like Siren kiss a man without needing a drink to wash her memory from my mind. I will never be able to kiss enough women to rid my brain of her kisses.

Why?

I don't know.

It's not love I'm feeling. Even though I've never loved a

woman before, I know that isn't what this is. If I was in love with her, I wouldn't have been able to watch her walk into that hotel room with him. I wouldn't have been able to pause outside for even a minute without chasing after and shooting him dead.

If it's not love, then what is it?

Lust?

Desire?

My claim that Siren is mine?

Fuck, I don't know.

I don't want love. I don't want some romantic fairytale that will never exist between us. The romantic gestures are just that—gestures. I'm a nice guy who likes taking care of others. I like flowering Siren with pretty things and then watching her squirm in discomfort, just like she likes kissing other men and watching the turmoil on my face.

I try to force myself to turn around. Let her fuck Beckett and kill him. Then I don't have to worry about him. I'll have accomplished Julian's sin without having to do anything.

I turn away.

I take a step.

And then I spin on a dime and run in the other direction.

I head into the hotel lobby, knowing it's too late to find out which room they are in by stalking them. My choices are to ask the hotel receptionist or hack the security system.

I stare at the hotel receptionist—a woman in her mid-twenties, already eating me up in my suit.

Flirting with the hotel receptionist it is.

"May I help you?" she asks in a too-sweet voice.

"Yes," I walk over and give her my best worried, puppy dog eyes. "My sister is diabetic. She left the bar with a date. She texted me this address and told me to bring her medicine, but her phone's dead, so I don't know which room to bring it to."

She smiles. "You are such a good big brother."

I lean on the counter until my hand just touches hers. She shivers like a thrill just shot through her. "I am."

"What's her last name?" she asks.

"I think the hotel is listed under her date's name, but I don't know his name. She probably got here five, maybe ten minutes before I did," I ask, hopeful she saw them enter together and knows who I'm talking about. I don't bother giving his name since I doubt he rented a room under it.

She frowns, trying to rack her brain.

"She was wearing tight jeans and a black shirt. He was in flannel and only has one arm."

"Oh, yes. I think he's on the eighth floor. But I'm not sure which room. Without his last name, I can't look him up."

I sigh. "Thanks."

I knock on five doors before I find the right one.

Siren answers the door, holding a glass of whiskey in her hand. Her pants are still on, but her shirt is off, giving me a perfect view of her black lace bra, pushing her boobs up.

"Going to accuse me of being a whore?" she asks, putting her hand on her hip clearly annoyed with me, when I should be the one annoyed with her.

I push past her and go inside; I'm not going to argue with her with the door open and Beckett inside.

I don't know what I expected when I walked inside, but what I find isn't it. Beckett is lying on the bed, slumped over, with his arm tied to the bedpost. His flannel shirt is open, but otherwise, he's completely dressed.

"Or accuse me of being into BDSM?" she asks, slamming the hotel room door.

I turn, and Siren runs into my body, the glass swaying in her hands.

"No, I was just going to say I was wrong."

She blinks rapidly, her mouth falling open slightly. "What do you mean, you were wrong?"

I take the glass from her hands, down it, and set it on the nightstand.

She frowns, crossing her arms, which only pushes her boobs up higher, distracting me.

"I'm waiting," she says when I don't answer.

"I was wrong when I said I don't want to be with you. When I said you were a whore. Or at least, implied it. I don't care who you are. I don't care what you've done. Or what the consequences are. I need to fuck you again."

Her tongue sticks out between her teeth at my words. And I can see so much happening behind her long eyelashes. Emotions I can't even begin to understand.

"You don't get to fuck me again. You had your one time."

"Liar," I say, stepping forward into her space.

She doesn't yield. She holds her ground and stares at Beckett instead of me.

I grab her chin, forcing her to look at me. "Don't look at him; look at me."

She exhales slowly as she looks at me.

"You've had us both. Tasted us both with your lips."

She nods.

"Who was better?"

"You," she whispers.

Heaven, it sounds like heaven hearing her confirm what I already know. Because she can't fake a kiss like ours. I know how incredibly rare it is. She doesn't kiss every man like that. I saw how she kissed Beckett. It was nothing compared to our kisses.

"You tasted his abs. Whose are better?" I ask, after I saw her red lipstick smeared on his chest.

She bites her teeth, holding back a sassy grin. "His."

I step further into her space. "I'm going to make you pay for that. Was that the first lie you ever told?"

She laughs gently, still on edge about what is happening between us. "It wasn't a lie; he has clearly spent more time on his abs than you have. But your arms…"

I growl, my arms definitely win as does another body part.

"Truth or sin? Who do you want to fuck? Him or me?"

She holds her breath, trying to figure a way out of this mess. The only way she ends this is to choose him. But that would be a lie, and she doesn't have it in her to lie, not with her words.

"You first. Truth or sin? Did you lie in our game earlier when you said you want to fuck Nora?"

I grab her wrists, and then I slam them high over her head as I push her body against the wall until she's trapped by my body. She can deny not liking giving up control all she wants, but I can read the signs. When it comes to sex, she wants to be controlled, dominated. She doesn't want nice. And good thing, because in the bedroom, I'm anything but nice.

"I didn't lie," I say.

Her eyes fall closed, and I can feel the pain emanating off her.

"But I didn't tell the complete truth either," I say.

Her eyes fly open.

"Yes, my cock would love to fuck Nora in the same way it wants to fuck any good looking woman. But not nearly as bad as I want to fuck you. If given the choice between fucking a hundred women or only you, I'd always choose you."

Her eyes heat, and her thoughts swirl in her head. She doesn't speak. She pants as she takes in every word I say.

"Truth or sin? Who do you want to fuck? Beckett or me?"

"Sin," she answers.

And I push up against her until she can feel every part of my hardness pushed up against her softness. Until I already know what sin she is planning on committing. She may not have chosen me with her words, but she's going to choose me with every other fiber of her being.

I lower my lips to hers, needing to taste her more than I need to breathe. Her lips part, ready for the kiss, wanting it desperately. But just before our lips touch, she says, "You, I don't want to fuck anyone but you."

Together we close the gap between us. Fuck, this kiss is better than I remember. The softness of her lips, the slickness of her tongue, the way she demands everything from me. I've never felt anything like her. I can't control my body, my thoughts, my wicked desires. She consumes everything within my body when she kisses me.

I trail my kisses down her neck, needing to taste every inch of her. She arches her back as I kiss, moaning as I continue to hold her against the wall. I can't let her go. I'll take her right here against the wall.

I grab her leg, pulling it up as I press between her.

"If you keep that up, I'm going to come before we get undressed," she moans.

"Good, I want to hear you scream my name a hundred times tonight."

My cock pushes up against her again, telling her exactly what I want from her, and what I plan on giving her.

"Fuck," she moans.

I smirk, pushing her bra down and finding her nipple to devour in my mouth. I'm rewarded with a delicious moan, and her twisting in my grasp, needing to get free and feel more of me.

"Are you going to fuck me against this wall?" Siren asks, raising an eyebrow at me.

"No, I want to fuck you in a bed." I grab her around the waist, pulling her from the wall and moving toward the bed when I suddenly remember Beckett is on the bed.

I howl.

She whimpers. "Zeke, I need—"

I devour her mouth again; I can't fuck her on the bed or even in this room, not with Beckett passed out on the bed. I should be focused on him. I should be searching his room and interrogating him before killing him and figuring out how to dispose of his body. Instead, all I can think about is Siren.

"Should we sneak into another hotel room?" I ask, not able to wait until after we get rid of Beckett to have her.

She gasps. "I can't wait that long."

Our hands move all over each other's bodies. Our tongues continue dancing and exploring each other's mouths, but it's not enough. We both want more. And I'm not going to let the fact that Beckett is lying on the only bed in the room stop us.

We both get the idea at the same time. We push through the bathroom door—my desire burning in my eyes, and Siren's need looming on her face.

I sweep the contents off the sink and counter in one swoop, and then I grab Siren and sit her up on the ledge.

My head dips back to her breasts, finding her nipple and teasing each peak as she unbuttons her pants. I grab them and yank them off her body before I kneel down and kiss the folds between her legs, pushing her panties aside. She's so wet, so sweet, so everything I want but have denied myself for too long. Once was never going to be enough when it came to Siren.

She grabs onto my hair, like she needs to hold onto me for balance, to stay grounded here in this moment as I bring her closer to the brink of her orgasm. Just as I know she's about to explode, she yanks my hair hard. And my lips fall away from Siren's body.

"What?" I growl, needing to hear her come, to taste her sweetness spill onto my tongue.

"I don't want to come until you're inside me. I want to save all my orgasms for when I can feel you, all of you."

Fuck. Yes.

She grins, her eyes heavy and seductive as she grabs onto the collar of my shirt. "Now, it's time I get you out of these ridiculous clothes."

"Ridiculous?" I nibble on her bottom lip as she starts undoing the buttons of my shirt. "Because from the attention you have been giving me all night, I figured you quite liked me in a suit."

She pushes the jacket off, then rips the rest of the buttons off as she tears my shirt open.

"I like you every way, but my preferred way is naked," she says before she sinks her nails into my chest, feeling every ripple of muscle on my chest and stomach.

I grab her hand, kissing her palm gently. "I thought you didn't like my abs? My abs aren't good enough?"

She bites her lip. "I just haven't gotten as acquainted with them as I want. I don't know them well enough." She leans forward and runs her tongue over each ripple, moving down further and further until her tongue dips just below the waistband of my pants.

"Jesus Christ," I curse, and then I come undone.

I'm tired of games. I'm tired of pretending we don't want each other when we do. Most of all, I'm tired of not having her when my entire body would give up food, water, and even its ability to breathe in order to have her.

"Fuck me, Zeke. Please, I can't wait."

I grab her off the counter and spin her around, pushing her down until she's hugging the sink with her arms, and her ass is in the air. She's still wearing her bra, and I'm still wearing my shirt ripped open and my pants. But neither of us can wait any longer to get fully undressed. Our need is too great.

I undo my pants, and my cock springs free already pushing at her entrance, knowing it's exactly where he belongs.

Our eyes lock in the mirror, and she spreads her legs wider for me. Her lips part, and her eyes darken, more than prepared for me. I want to take my time, knowing that each time I have her could be my last. But I can't control myself. Not with her.

I grab her hips and sink inside her as she pushes back against me.

"Tell me you want me," I say as I thrust in her.

"I want you. I want this."

"Tell me this isn't your sin? That this won't be the last time we fuck."

She gasps as I push deeper inside her, and then her eyelashes flutter up. "This won't be the last time."

Yes.

She said it, so it will be true.

Because this can't be the last time, I need so much more. I need her on all fours, on top of me, spread on my bed. I need her slow and fast. I need her on the counter, in the shower, on the bed, against the wall, and every other surface I can find. I need her tied up and in control.

I need Siren in every way before I can let her go.

Fucking her now is only the start.

"Harder, Zeke," Siren cries out.

I fuck her slower, not ready to let her come just yet. I know that her pulsing around me, combined with her screaming my name, will make me come far faster than I want.

"Zeke!" Her cries beg me to move faster, to give her what she needs—an explosive orgasm.

I take my time, drawing everything out. "Not yet, my siren. Not yet."

She claws at the sink, and from the dirty look she's giving me, she wishes her nails were driving into my flesh, telling me exactly how desperately she wants me to stop teasing her and let her come.

But when I thrust inside her again, my patience evaporates. I need to come as badly as she does.

So I move harder, faster, gripping her hips as I thrust in and out of her. Her pussy throbs on my cock, telling me how close she is. Her little whimpers push me forward. She whips her hair from her back to shoulder and flashes me a look that reads sin. I reach around her body, finding her clit with my fingers. She shudders at the touch and then...

She sings my name at the top of her lungs.

And I'm hers in an instant. I want a repeat of this moment, now and forever. I don't know about forever, but I can settle on now.

21

SIREN

WHEN ZEKE FUCKS ME, it feels like he belongs in me. Like he's the missing piece of my puzzle.

And the second he stops, I feel alone and desperate. I feel empty—not just physically, but like he takes all of the life inside me with him when he stops.

I stand gripping the sink, my legs weak, and my body trembling. Zeke is standing behind me, staring at me like he can't believe what just happened, and he's not sure what to do next.

I'm not sure either. This wasn't supposed to happen. We were only supposed to fuck once. Now that we've fucked a second time, what is going to stop us from doing it over and over again? Even if I know how this ends—us hating each other even more than we already do.

I take a deep, steadying breath as I look at Zeke in the mirror. He's looking at me with hungry, determined eyes. We fucked so quickly, neither of us is even fully undressed. He's still wearing his pants and shirt. I'm still wearing my bra and panties he pushed to the side when we fucked.

But neither of us look more satiated than we did before we started.

"We should go check on Beckett," I say between heavy breaths crashing through my entire body.

"Should we?" Zeke asks, running his fingers down my back.

I nod.

I watch as he shrugs off his shirt and then steps out of his pants until he's naked. My tongue flicks to the roof of my mouth, trying desperately to not show him how his naked body affects me.

He steps back, keeping his eyes on me, he opens the glass door and flicks on the shower.

"Or?" he cocks his head to the side, with a devious twinkle in his eyes, telling me what he wants without saying it.

So I respond the same way. I unhook my bra, letting it fall down my arms. Then I slide my black panties down before stepping out of my heels.

I take a step toward him, feeling seductive, but my legs are weakened. I grip the sink, keeping myself standing as the effects of my early orgasm roll through me. Zeke took everything from me when he fucked me.

He smirks at my reaction.

He steps forward and grabs my arm, tugging me to him. And then he pulls me into the shower.

"I can never get enough of you," he says, before his lips claim mine again.

And when he kisses me, that's exactly how I feel—claimed. Like he's demanding me to say I'm his with each kiss. Say I belong to him.

I don't want to belong to anyone. I don't want to be

claimed. Even if a tiny part of my heart aches to be his. I won't let that part of me win. I will never belong to anyone but myself. Not again.

Zeke kisses me again, and I falter. I stop the kiss, letting my face fall as the water hits my face, smacking me with reality. I need a moment to think, to clear my head.

But Zeke doesn't let me pause. He tilts my head up, until our eyes meet again, and he presses a soft kiss. "It's only sex."

It's only sex. It's what I want to hear and also the same words that will destroy me. His words should be exactly what I want to hear. Instead, they rip me down to my soul.

He deepens his kisses, reminding my body of how badly I want him. And I forget about his words. I forget about everything else except Zeke. My body stirs, needing him again.

He's gentle with me this time. He holds me up against the wall as my legs continue to tremble from exhaustion, but not willing to give up having him again. I want him. I need him. And shaky legs will not stop me from having him.

I pull his hair free from the man bun, and he shakes his hair as the water runs over us both. My back shivers against the cool tile, and Zeke kisses every inch of my body he can find—my neck, my breasts, my stomach. He stops between my thighs when I gasp from a single kiss there.

After our first round, I'm so sensitive that I could burst from a single touch.

But then he lowers his mouth, kissing over the wound that has only started to heal on my leg. And I can read his pain in his eyes.

"This is just sex, remember?" I say to him, not able to handle his pity.

"Just sex," he says back before kissing my scar again.

I gasp at the sensitive brush of his lips over my thigh. He continues over all of my body, trying to kiss every scar he can find like he's kissing away the memory of each pain inflicted. He doesn't realize the only scar on my body that needs healing is the one over my heart. But that scar is unhealable.

I start to shiver again, and Zeke holds me tight to his body, warming me. I feel the hardness of his chest against my cheek, I feel his heart beating against my ear, and I belong here, in his arms.

Zeke kisses down my face, and then without speaking, he lifts one of my legs, and he enters me in one long stroke.

I gasp as he fills me.

It's a feeling I'm not sure I'll ever get used to when it comes to Zeke, or want to ever give up.

I wrap my hands around his neck, and we kiss lazily like we've been kissing each other our entire lives as Zeke slides in and out of me. He moves like he knows every curve of my body and what every whimper escaping my throat means. And he does.

He shouldn't be able to make me feel so good, not when he's being so casual. He shouldn't know my body so well. But it seems he's discovered all of my secrets, at least my physical ones.

We move together in unison, both taking our time, building to the inevitable moment this ends.

I gasp and pant and feel my nerves tingling with excitement. And I know I'm about to come. I bite down on Zeke's shoulder, causing a tiny droplet of his blood to flee as I pierce his flesh.

The roar he gives me in return hits me right in the gut.

When he comes, I feel his warm seed inside me. When he pulls out, I feel it flow down my leg. And for a moment, I feel so incredibly content. If I keep fucking him, I could chase this feeling for much longer.

Slowly, Zeke puts my leg down, making sure I'm steady on my feet.

This was just sex.

He reaches behind him and grabs the shampoo bottle. I put my hand out to take it from him when he's finished. Instead, he squirts the shampoo on my head and massages it into my scalp with his magical fingers.

I close my eyes, getting lost in how good his hands make me feel. I've never been pampered before, but I guess this is how it feels. Zeke washes my hair, then my body.

When I open my eyes, he has a fluffy towel wrapped around me. I realize this is more than just sex. I don't know what it is. I don't know when Zeke stopped hating me entirely for my betrayal. I don't know when I stopped thinking about him as only my enemy. But it happened.

And now this is happening. Zeke is taking care of me, and I didn't immediately fight him off. This new relationship we have entered into is going to fuck up everything, because it sure as hell isn't just sex. It's definitely not love, we aren't dating, but it's more than just sex.

I wrap the towel around my body and step out without speaking a word to Zeke. There are no words to say. Everything has changed, and although the sex is out of this world amazing, the consequences are going to be equally damaging.

I pick up my bra and ruined panties off the floor. Then find my jeans and shoes. I put everything on except for the panties, while Zeke dries off and wraps the towel around his waist, in no hurry to get dressed.

I wring my hair out, knowing it's going to be a frizzy mess in an hour when it air dries, but I don't want to stay in the bathroom with Zeke just so I can dry my hair.

I run out of the bathroom to find my shirt and wait for Zeke to get dressed. Hopefully, we will get back to business. We will figure out what to do with Beckett, and then when we return to St. Kitts, we will continue to hate each other.

I bend down and pick up my shirt off the floor of the bedroom. And I pause.

"Zeke!" I shout.

He runs out, still only wearing the towel. His eyes are wide, and his teeth clenched.

I run my hand through my hair in frustration.

Beckett is gone. He snuck out while we were fucking.

"We need to start going through his things, see if we can find any clues to where he's gone," Zeke snaps.

I nod.

But as I look around the room, I realize we didn't just make one mistake; we made two. Clothes hang off every piece of furniture in the room. But there is no flannel, no jeans, no men's clothes at all. The room is filled with women's clothes. And before we fucked on it, the bathroom vanity was covered in makeup.

"This isn't Beckett's room," I say to Zeke as he opens a drawer in the nightstand.

Zeke stands up, examining the room closely, and realizing I've spoken the truth.

"Dammit," he says, kicking the nightstand so hard it falls over. He's glaring at me like this is all my fault. Like I tricked him somehow by forcing him to fuck me.

I glare back. I won't let him blame me.

I pull on my shirt and untuck my hair out from my neckline, flipping it to one side.

"I'm going to find Beckett. When you stop glaring, come find me." I throw the door open. "Or don't." I stomp outside and slam the door in Zeke's face, knowing that fucking Zeke just became an even bigger mistake.

It could cost Zeke everything, if we don't find Beckett.

22

ZEKE

I'M SUCH A FOOL. That's how I feel every time I let Siren back into my life. *I'm a fucking fool.*

I should have been focused on Beckett. Instead, I was tempted by Siren. And once I was under her spell, there was nothing to break me free of her. Fucking her again made me realize that with one kiss, she can manipulate me into doing anything. One fuck, and I would risk my life for her.

It was a mistake.

Kissing her.

Fucking her.

All of it.

And now I'm alone in a hotel room, with only a towel around my waist. Siren has run off, and I'm not sure if it's to bail me out of this mess by finding Beckett or to abandon me and make me figure it out by myself.

I head back to the bathroom to retrieve my clothes, and all the memories and emotions of just a few minutes ago come flooding back. The way Siren looked at me, the way she moaned for me, the way she felt around my cock.

Fucking her might have been a mistake, but it was worth it.

I throw my clothes on, not even bothering to button my shirt up as I chase after Siren. I run through the hotel and take the stairs instead of the elevator, hoping Siren didn't get very far in the time it took me to get my head together.

But I don't find her in the lobby or on the street.

I run my hand through my long hair in frustration. A burst of thunder rolls overhead, and I shudder as rain pours down on me, matching my mood. I'm wet, half-dressed, and bewildered as to the locations of either Beckett or Siren.

It doesn't get much worse.

I feel a buzz in my pocket, and I yank my phone out to a text message from Siren.

Got a car. Meet me at the corner of 10th and Cummings.

I sigh and rub my neck. Siren is always two steps ahead of me. I need to think faster if I'm ever going to keep up with her.

I jog the three blocks to the corner she described. Two seconds later, a Toyota pulls up next to me.

I move to grab the passenger door when the driver's side door opens, and Siren pops out, flicking me the keys. I catch them with a puzzled look.

"You're letting me drive?" I ask.

She sighs. "Just drive. I'll explain when we aren't both getting soaked."

We both run around the car until I'm on the driver's side, and she's on the passenger's side. We climb in, and I start driving, even though I don't have a clue where I'm going.

"Where am I driving?"

"Straight. I'm tracking him on my phone," Siren says.

I glance over at her. "You're tracking Beckett?"

"Yes, I put a tracker on his phone while he was out. But if he's smart, he'll ditch his phone soon. So we need to hurry."

I nod and step on it, making her grip her seat and inhale a deep breath. I'm surprised she's riding in the car with me driving again.

"He's at the docks," Siren says.

I take a sharp turn and head toward the docks.

An awkward silence passes now that we have nothing to talk about until we get there.

"I'm not going to apologize," Siren says.

I stiffen.

"I did nothing wrong," she says.

I pull the car over to the side of the road as we reach the docks.

"You never do."

I don't know if I meant it honestly or sarcastically, but by the scowl on her face, I know the words came out wrong.

I'm a stupid fool. But right now, I can't apologize for it or convince Siren I didn't mean anything by it. Right now, I need to find Beckett.

I pull my gun out as I jump out of the car.

Siren does the same next to me.

"You don't need to come. I got this," I say.

"Sexist," she murmurs under her breath.

"No, you are more than capable of defending yourself. This just isn't your fight. It's mine. And as you don't want me to protect you, I don't want to be protected either."

She frowns. "I can help."

"I know. But don't."

She follows me for another second toward the docks and

then stops.

I continue on my own, not looking back at Siren. She's safe, that's all that matters.

The sky is dark, well past midnight. There are no lamp posts on the long pier I'm walking down. The only light is from the moon overhead and the lights from the town behind me. But the darkness doesn't stop me from walking. I need to find Beckett. I need to complete the first sin.

And I need to get Siren out of my fucking head.

I don't see any movement or hear sounds of other men as I walk. I feel completely alone. It's how I like it when I go into battle. Alone, so I have no one to protect except myself.

I keep walking into the darkness, hoping Siren is right, and Beckett is here. Hoping he didn't just throw his phone out the window and keep driving.

A red light blinds me and gives me my answer.

I freeze, as the red light trains on my forehead.

"Put your hands up," Beckett says from the darkness.

I don't know how good of a shot he is, but I do as he says while he has his gun aimed at my forehead. I'm guessing he can at least hit me when I'm out in the wide open, and there is little to no pressure on him.

"Drop the gun," Beckett says, as he steps out of the shadows.

I reluctantly do as he says again. He's several feet away from me. Too far for me to disarm him. And he'd shoot me dead before I was able to aim my gun in his direction. I could try to jump over the side into the water, but my chances of him not hitting me are slim. My only shot is talking him down.

"We should talk," I say.

Beckett laughs. "You want to talk, huh? Right, now that you are the one about to be shot, you want to talk. But when your girlfriend drugged me and tied me up, you didn't seem to be in much of a talking mood."

I take a deep breath, trying to figure out how to get out of here alive. At least if Beckett kills me, Julian will never get any information about Enzo Black. He will never learn how to take him down. He will remain safe.

"Where is your girlfriend?" Beckett asks.

"She's not my girlfriend. And she's not involved in this life at all."

"Maybe not, but she's clearly a pro."

I shrug. "Who cares if she is? She's working for me. I'm the one who wants you dead, not her."

"Who do you work for?" Beckett asks.

"Myself."

Beckett frowns. "And who are you? You say you work for yourself, then who are you?"

"I'm Zeke Kane."

He blinks rapidly. "Zeke Kane is dead. You're an imposter. Trying to use his connections and likeness. Tell me who you really are, or I'll kill you."

I narrow my eyes, my hands still in the air, and his gun still aimed at my head. This man knows who I am. He knows my name. He knows I'm supposed to be dead. But I have no clue who he is. I don't remember him from my life before.

"Three..." Beckett starts.

"Really? Going to countdown like I'm a child? You think that's going to work?" I joke, hoping it will get him to stop long enough so I can think about what to do next. *How do I find out who he is? How do I keep him from shooting me first?*

"Two."

Fuck.

"One."

I close my eyes, readying myself for death. I've already escaped death so many times before. Fate is finally going to win.

"Wait!" I hear a desperate voice scream from the darkness—Siren's wail.

I open my eyes and find her standing next to me, completely out of breath, her body trembling, and her eyes wild with pain.

She doesn't care about me. She's just acting.

"Don't kill him. I'll tell you everything you need to know," Siren says.

Beckett's eyes go between Siren and me, but he keeps the gun pointed at me. *Good.*

"And why should I listen to you?" Beckett asks.

"Because I'm Aria Torres." *Wait...she told me before her last name was Martinez? Did she lie to me then? Or is she lying now?*

Beckett immediately aims his gun at Aria instead of me.

She smirks with her hands on her hips, and I see the relief on her face now that the gun is no longer pointed at me.

"Zeke works for me. Take me, not him," she says.

"Done," Beckett says.

Siren starts walking forward, but I grab her arm. "No," I say.

She rips her wrist from my grasp. "Save yourself, don't come after me. Swear it?"

I don't swear. And then she walks over to Beckett while he continues to aim the gun at her.

"Follow me, and I'll kill her," Beckett says.

She saved me when I didn't deserve saving.

But if she thinks I can just let Beckett take her without fighting back, then she doesn't know me at all. I will never make that vow.

23

SIREN

BECKETT KEEPS the gun aimed at me as I step onto a small dingy boat, and we speed off. And I resist the urge to look back to the pier to see if Zeke heeded my warning and left, or if he's still standing there, trying to figure out how to save me.

I don't want to know which he chose. Either option would gut me.

"Put your hands up," Beckett says.

I do.

He stops the boat after we've traveled at least a mile away from shore. He pats me down, finding my gun and knife, before tying my arms behind my back with rope. He does quite a good job for a man with only one arm.

With us a mile from shore, I finally glance back at the pier. I can no longer make out people. I can barely make out the pier jutting out into the water. So I have no idea what Zeke decided to do.

But at least in this moment, he's safe. Watching him stand on the pier, defending those he loved, was astonishing. It was an incredible sight of courageousness. *And it fucking terrified me.*

Once Zeke started down the pier, I tried to stay back and do what he asked. But I couldn't stand by and watch him die. I just couldn't. Even if we are enemies. Even if he's destined to kill me one day.

I've never felt so terrified. My body shook with fear, thinking I might not run down the pier fast enough in my heels to stop Beckett from shooting him dead.

And when I saved him, it was like the sun came out again for the first time. I wasn't going to have to live a life cast in darkness, a life without Zeke.

Once Beckett has my arms tied and my weapons taken, he sits back, staring at me. "So you're the famous Aria Torres, man-eater."

I nod. "I'm surprised you didn't figure it out when I told you my first name."

He rests his gun in his lap as he studies me. "I fell for your charm, same as every other man you've encountered. But you're getting soft. You should have shot and killed me in that hotel room, not tied me up and fucked another man. That was careless of you."

"It was."

"So why didn't you kill me then?"

"Because I wanted to question you first, with Zeke's help."

"What questions could you possibly have?"

I smile. "None anymore. You already answered my question."

"And what question was that?"

"Who are you?"

He stills.

"You're Eli Beckett. You work for the Black empire."

His jaw tenses, and his shoulders flex, ready to fight. I thought my comment might get me shot on the spot, but Beckett knows he needs to find out who I work for, or who I've passed that information along to first.

Beckett made it very hard for me to find out who his boss is, which means Mr. Black uses Beckett for secret operations. So knowing his identity would put his job at risk.

"How do you know that?" Beckett finally asks. He doesn't raise his gun. He knows I'll answer without threatening him. Because only one of us is going to survive this boat ride. So there is no danger in us both spilling our secrets.

"Because you know Zeke Kane."

"I don't actually."

Now it's my turn to raise an eyebrow. "You sure seemed like it back there."

"I know the name. I know Zeke Kane used to work for my boss. I also know that he died. But I never met the man. Just heard great things about him."

Ah, there it is. "So you have no idea if the man you almost killed was the actual Zeke Kane or an imposter?"

He nods slowly.

I laugh and lean forward. "Well, let me let you in on a secret. That man back there, is the real Zeke Kane. He survived. I was the one who saved him. I pulled him from the water. You almost shot the wrong guy."

"Fuck," Beckett says, leaning back in his chair in complete shock.

He rubs his temple. "But if that is really Zeke, the infamous man who laid down his life to save people time and time again, then why is he working for you?"

Because I have the ability to control his heart. "Why do you think?"

"Because he's trying to protect the Black family. Same as always."

Bingo.

"Jesus, I guess I should thank you," he says.

"For what?"

"For keeping me from making the biggest mistake of my life. If I killed Zeke, no one would ever forgive me."

Least of all me.

"So are the rumors true? Can you really kill a man with just one look?" he asks.

"You tell me." I swing my still damp hair over my shoulder and push out my breasts as I carefully move my fingers down, where I dropped a weapon into the darkness of the boat before Beckett searched me.

He frowns. "I don't know what to make of you, Aria. But I think you are worthy of every rumor that has ever been told about you."

I smile. "Thanks for the compliment."

"Do you work alone or for someone?" he asks.

"I work for myself." And that statement has never been more true. I work for myself. Everything I do is selfish. Even if Julian Reed likes to claim the title of boss. There is so much more to the truth than that.

"What's your plan now? What do you want with me?" I ask, licking my lip, teasing him with my tongue, and reminding him of our kiss, even though I know that moment has passed. *Sex won't save me this time.*

"You already know what I have to do. I have to kill you. You're a threat to me, my boss, and even Zeke. I have to kill you and go rescue Zeke."

I take a deep breath. "That's my move."

My words are a warning. My eyes flick wide with urgency. And then I jump at the same time Beckett does. We both dive in opposite directions, moments before the bomb goes off. Water sprays my face as I dive under the water. I kick hard to get as far away from the explosion.

And when the explosion hits, I'm deep below the water. But I still feel the explosion vibrate through me. I don't look for Beckett under the water, but I have no doubt he survived.

I warned him; I shouldn't have. I should have killed him. It's what Julian wanted. But then again, I don't always do what Julian wants. I just pay when I refuse to follow his commands.

24

ZEKE

I WATCHED Siren get on a boat with Beckett pointing a gun at her head, and I did nothing. I didn't have a choice; he would have shot her if I made a move. But it was still almost impossible to stand there, instead of sprint after her.

As soon as the boat got far enough away, I jumped into the nearest speed boat and hot-wired it. Then I took off.

Siren told me to save myself. I should. I should turn around and drive this boat as far away from here as possible.

Beckett told me if I followed him, he'd kill Siren. But his words don't stop me either.

I'm tired of not knowing the truth. I'm tired of Siren confusing the heck out of me. She shouldn't have saved me. She should have let Beckett kill me. Then she could have killed Beckett and gone back to Julian as a hero. And she would no longer have to deal with me.

But she didn't let me die. She saved me.

And as I speed out into the ocean, I guess that's what I'm doing—saving her.

I lose sight of them as they round the corner of a small island.

But a few minutes later, I hear a loud boom before they come into view. There is no way to miss them. The small boat is on fire, smoke billowing out of it. Neither of them is still on the boat, if they survived. They would have burned to ash in the explosion.

I turn off the engine as I watch the flames slowly burn out. My heart stops, my breath extinguishes. And my eyes water at the sight.

Siren's dead.

She died instead of me.

It should have been me!

I wipe the tears on the back of my hand as I start the engine again. *No, she can't be dead.* I start the engine up and am about to speed off again when I hear the most incredible voice.

"You trying to save me again? I told you I don't need saving," Siren says.

I let out a stifled laugh that's half cry and half pure joy, as tears fall down my face. I wipe them quickly before I turn, hoping she won't see how much emotion she pulled out of me.

I clear my throat to prevent some high pitched squeak before I speak. "I wasn't coming to save you. I came to finish the job." I nod in the direction of the fire. "But it seems like you took care of Beckett yourself."

Her eyes glisten, and I wonder if she's teared up as well. But it's impossible to tell in the night.

"Zeke, I—"

But I stop her from speaking when I yank her out of the water and pull her into the deepest hug. She's soaking wet, and I swear I hear sobs into my shoulder as I hold her.

I may have questions I need answered, and she may have

truths she needs to tell. But right now, I need a moment just to celebrate the fact that she's not dead.

Holding her in my arms isn't enough, though. And apparently, it isn't enough for her either.

"Zeke, I need—" she lets out a deep breath instead of finishing that sentence.

And man, do I want her to finish that sentence. But I want to feel connected to her even more. And if physically is the only way she will let me connect with her, then so be it.

"Kiss me," I demand.

And she does. She tilts her head up, stands on her tiptoes, and kisses me with everything she has. Her tongue pushes into my mouth with great efficiency. She knows exactly what she wants from me. And she's not afraid to take it. I guess almost dying makes things clearer in one's head. At least, it does me.

I run my hands down her arms, realizing that the reason her hands aren't all over my body is because they are tied behind her back. My hands fist in anger at the thought of another man tying her up. Trying to control her. She's mine.

But my conscience is laughing at me for thinking a woman like Siren could ever be claimed, or could ever belong to a man. She's the kind of woman who will only ever belong to herself.

I slowly spin Siren around, who whimpers when I force her to break the kiss. I have fantasies of tying Siren up every which way in my bed. But I'm not going to fulfill any of them with her arms tied by another man.

I pull a knife from my pocket and slice through the ropes, freeing her hands.

"I'm the only one allowed to tie you up," I whisper into her ear. "You're mine."

And the beautiful exhale that escapes her lips tells me she agrees.

She shivers, cold, and soaked in her clothes.

I wrap my arms around her, needing her warm.

"There are better ways to keep me warm," she pants.

I nuzzle her neck and then press a sweet kiss to her neck. "Yea? What are you thinking?"

She turns her head and kisses me, hard like she needs the kiss in order to stay alive. "Fuck me, Zeke."

God, how I'll never tire of hearing her say that. But I want answers.

"Truth or sin?" I ask.

She nods.

But then she kisses me again, and I forget about our game. It's not a game either of us need in order to fuck anymore. We are going to need to change the rules to get each other to spill truths, since we'd both rather commit a sin together.

She shoves me back onto the bench in the middle of the boat, and I sit as she straddles me.

I grab the hem of her shirt and peel it off, watching as the goosebumps spring up all over her delicate skin. She wastes no time unhooking her bra. I'm sure it's uncomfortable being soaking wet, but it's not the only reason she's removing it. She wants assurance that I fuck her no matter what questions I ask or truths she answers. And sitting naked on my lap is definitely a guarantee.

"You're incredible. You saved yourself from an explosion. You swam with your arms tied up. I've never met a woman quite like you."

She leans down, grabbing my head as she kisses me. "I caused the explosion. That's how I saved myself."

And then she kisses me, and I feel every bit of that explosion in my mouth, against my tongue. Her hands dip beneath my shirt, shoving it open, ripping the remaining buttons from our last romp off my shirt. Her hands feel amazing, but I'm not going to let her avoid answering my questions.

"Why can't you lie?" I ask, holding her back, refusing to let her kiss me without answering.

She opens her mouth, probably to say sin. "If you choose sin, trust me—you won't like it."

The only way she is going to get me to fuck her is by answering my question. When it's her turn to ask a question, I will answer it truthfully no matter what she asks, refusing her a sin.

She realizes it in my eyes. *But does she want to fuck me badly enough to tell me a truth?*

"It started when I was a girl."

I feel the pain in her voice when she speaks.

"My parents hated it when I lied. So they made sure I was appropriately punished every time they caught me in a lie."

"Your scars?"

"Some of them were caused by my parents."

"And the others?"

"That's not part of your question."

I sigh.

"What keeps you from lying now?"

She runs her nail over my chest. "Most of the reason is I can't. Part of the emotional trauma from my childhood of literally getting beaten every time I lied."

"And the other part?"

"A vow I made to a man never to lie."

"To who?"

"You already know the answer."

Julian Reed.

I want to ask more, but I've pushed enough. She answered my question, and I got another piece of her puzzle. I know what my next question will be, and I just hope that I can get her to answer and not choose sin.

She exhales a breath when she realizes I'm done asking my question. *Your turn, Siren.*

"Where is Enzo Black?"

Her question isn't a fair one. It makes me hate her. It makes me distrust her. And it makes me think the only way to save Enzo and my friends is to eventually kill her.

But she's also asking because she wants a sin. She doesn't realize that after her spilling her truth, I'll fuck her without needing her to earn a sin.

"Sin," I answer.

And with that, she steps back. She removes her pants, now naked in front of me. Her skin shimmers in the moonlight, still damp from the ocean water.

She steps forward, grabbing my jeans. She undoes the button and zipper and yanks them down.

My eyes roam her body as she stands in front of me. My cock is hard and straining to be inside her.

She grins seductively as she straddles me again, taking full control. This must be her sin, fucking me without letting me demand anything from her. She's going to take what she needs from my body without thinking about me, and I've never seen anything sexier.

When she sinks down on top of my cock, all my feelings come flooding back. Feelings I have no right to. I shouldn't fall for her in any single way. Not as friends or lovers. This is all a trick, just like before. She wants something from me, and she using my emotions to get it. *Not going to happen.*

But my cock gets lost in her pussy, thrusting in and out as our eyes lock wide open, while kissing each other. My heart flutters in my chest feeling her heart so close to mine. My brain may know who Siren is, but right now, it's having trouble explaining to my cock and heart how to feel.

Siren moves on top of me in careful, practiced movements. She doesn't let me do any of the work. She takes it all herself, pumping up and down over me. Her boobs bob up and down in front of my chest. Her hands grip my shoulders, and she moves herself up and down in a beautiful rhythm. The boat rocks as we do, and I get completely lost in her.

"Jesus, Siren, you're incredible. And you're mine."

She takes my pleasure for her own. And then we both crash, our bodies explode with each other, and it feels bigger than the explosion that happened moments before.

Slowly, Siren stops rocking over me. She climbs off, picking up my shirt off the floor. She puts it on, along with her jeans.

"What am I supposed to wear?" I ask.

She grins, tossing me my slacks. I guess I'm going shirtless. And it's worth it to see her wear my shirt.

I come up behind her and pull her to my chest. "That was one hell of a sin."

"That wasn't my sin."

"Oh?"

She reaches down and grabs the knife I used to untie her ropes with. She hands it to me. I take it looking at it in confusion.

Then she sits down on the bench and motions for me to sit behind her. I do.

She lifts her hair up in a ponytail.

"Carve your initials below Julian's," she says.

"What? Why would I do that?" I ask in disgust.

"Because I earned a sin."

I stare at her in disbelief. "No."

"You don't get to say no. I earned a sin. I get to choose anything. Now, do it."

Her voice shakes me. I've never seen her so determined. "Why?" And I know as soon as I ask it, it's the wrong question. And her answer is going to break me.

She looks me dead in the eyes. "Because I'm tired of men thinking they can own me. Tell me what to do. Or even save me. You think you can own me? Then mark me as yours, just like Julian."

I growl. "I'm nothing like Julian."

"You're exactly like him," she snaps.

"Not possible! I tried to save you, Julian would never do that! I've seen how he treats you. He hurts you over and over again. All I've ever done is try to be nice to you!"

"No! You try to save me, even when I tell you not to. Even when I plead for you not to. You have no idea the damage you've done. You have no idea I now belong to you as much as I belong to Julian."

I blink rapidly, not understanding. "What are you saying?"

"I'm telling you to carve your initials below Julian's. You already think of me as yours. You tell me I'm yours whenever we fuck. I'm telling you that you saved me one too many times. I'm telling you that you ruined my life! That you've taken from me too many times. So carve your damn initials into my neck, so I can remember you are not my friend, you're just trying to control me the same as Julian."

"No."

I drop the knife.

She picks it up with tears in her eyes I don't understand. Tears that say she's feeling more, but she's afraid, so damn afraid. "Carve your initials, or we are done. There will be no more truths. No more sins."

No more us.

Whatever that means. I don't know what *us* is.

Reluctantly, I take the knife.

She turns, holding her hair up for me. I see Julian's hastily carved initials and a faint outline of a different mark just above his, buried in her hair. I have a feeling carving my initials is more than what she is asking. There is more truth she isn't speaking—a reason she wants me to do this.

One reason is she knows hurting her will hurt me.

A second reason is she's scared of her own feelings for me. And this is a way she can stay angry instead of letting her feelings for me out.

And the third reason is yet to be discovered.

I press the knife carefully to her flesh, and then I carve my initials—ZK.

I watch myself hurt her. I watch the blood flow. I watch the pain I cause, and tears roll down my cheek.

When I've finished, she releases her hair. "That's what it feels like every time you try to save me. Every time you claim I'm yours. Every time you don't trust me. Like you are laying claim to something you have no right to earn." Her tears spring free until we are both crying in the back of the boat.

I open my mouth to say I'm sorry, but then I stop. Because I'm not sorry for saving her, or at least trying to. Just like she's not sorry she saved me. And I'm sure as hell not sorry for saying she's mine, even when I know she can never be.

Instead, I grab her and pull her tight to my chest, comforting her.

I look out at the sea and the wreckage of the boat. She survived. *Could Beckett have survived too?*

25

SIREN

I LET Zeke drive me back to the hotel. We don't speak after the sin I made him carry out, but it was an intense moment. A moment where I felt all my power return. I'm tired of men controlling my life.

Zeke parks the stolen car a block from the hotel. We step out, and I start walking up to the hotel in his shirt and my damp jeans. Zeke chases after me, still shirtless, only wearing his slacks and carrying his suit jacket.

He grabs my hand as we walk.

I try to pull my hand free.

But he only tightens his grip. "You can fight me all you want. But I'm bigger than you and as you made me carve into your neck, you're mine."

He's pissed I made him hurt me. But maybe he'll think twice now before playing that stupid game again or using it to get what he wants from me.

I'm exhausted, so I stop resisting, and we walk hand in hand through the lobby of the hotel and into the elevator. Once inside, I try to pull my hand away again, but he continues gripping it.

"You aren't in control anymore. I committed your sin," he growls.

The doors open on my floor, and Zeke drags me down the hallway. For a second I think, he's bringing me back to my hotel room to fuck me again, and my heart speeds up at the thought. But when he knocks on the door, and Nora opens it with her eyebrows raised, I realize he's just delivering me to my hotel room to ensure I don't get into any more trouble.

Zeke gives Nora a curt nod and pulls me inside.

"Nora, can you give us a minute?" Zeke mumbles, barely looking at her.

"Sure," she grabs her purse and then heads out the door.

Finally, I yank my hand free. "You can go, too. I don't need a babysitter."

He huffs. "You've run off on me enough times; it seems to be exactly what you need." He heads toward the bathroom. "Sit," he commands. The look on his face telling me that if I don't sit on the bed, he's going to return and spank me so hard I will no longer be able to sit.

So I sit.

I hear him rummage through drawers and cabinets in the bathroom, mumbling and cursing. Finally, he returns, carrying a small bandaid and washcloth.

"This is all I could find," he grumbles, holding the items up.

I sigh. Zeke can't stand not to help me.

"I don't need your help."

"I don't care what you need. You're going to take my help so I can sleep tonight."

"No, I'm not." I fold my arms across my chest.

"Yes, you are." His voice booms so loud I'm sure everyone in the hotel heard.

"If I let you, will you leave?"

"Yes."

I lift my hair and turn so he can see my neck. And then I feel him press the cool washcloth to his initials. It feels like heaven against my warm skin.

I melt just a little, sinking into the bed and into his hand pressing against my neck.

"You are the most stubborn woman I've ever met."

"And you are the most arrogant man."

He moves the washcloth, and I let out a low hiss as the sting jolts me.

"I'm sorry," he says softly, meaning every word.

But I don't want him to be sorry. For anything.

"I think the bleeding has stopped," he says a few minutes later.

I nod.

And then I hear him unwrapping the bandaid before he presses it to my skin.

"It's not big enough to cover the entire area, but at least your hair won't rub against it and irritate it."

I drop my hair back down.

"You should get out of those wet clothes," he commands.

"Turn around," I say, even though he just saw my naked body before. Right now, I'm angry at him, and he doesn't get to see me naked when I'm angry.

He turns, and I slip out of my wet jeans and heels. But I leave his T-shirt on.

"Okay," I say, when I've done as he said.

He turns. I expect him to tell me to give him his shirt back, but he doesn't. He acts like his shirt belongs on my body.

"Now get under the covers. You need to rest."

I don't want to be ordered around, but he's right. I need sleep. So I crawl into bed.

Zeke sits on the side of the bed, pulling the covers up tightly around me and tucking me in. He hesitates for a second and then asks, "Is Beckett dead?"

I knew he would ask. If I'm alive, Beckett could have survived the blast too. And I have to be careful with how I answer. Because when we return home, I'll be the proof Julian needs to know that Zeke did his job. I need to believe that Beckett is dead, whether he is or not.

And right now, I don't know.

"Beckett was on the boat when the bomb went off. What do you think?" I answer.

Zeke nods, accepting my answer. That answer won't fly with Julian. Julian knows all my tricks. He knows how I can answer without truly answering the question to avoid lying. He will want a yes or no. I need Zeke to get me to believe that he found evidence of Beckett's death in order to pass that information along to Julian. Whether Beckett actually died or not.

Zeke tucks my hair behind my ear. "Get some rest. Tomorrow we will head back to St. Kitts."

Zeke stands as Nora opens the door to the hotel room.

"Take care of her, Nora," Zeke says as he leaves.

Nora sets her purse down and then climbs up the bed next to me. "Want to talk about it?"

"No."

She sighs. "So you're telling me I can't have Zeke or Beckett?"

I throw a pillow at her.

"I was just asking," she says back. She stands up, pulls her dress off, and climbs under the covers, wrapping her arms around me. "I'm always here if you need a friend to talk to."

I nod and kiss her hand because Nora is a good friend. But I need more than someone to talk to if I'm going to fix the predicament I'm in. I need a way to stop letting men into my life.

26

ZEKE

I PULL on a shirt in my hotel room while thinking about Siren. She better stay in that damn bed tonight. I hope Nora will make sure she does.

Beckett is dead. I will never know who he worked for. *Did he work for Enzo Black? Was he an ally? Or was he an enemy?*

I toss my wallet on the nightstand and start kicking my shoes off.

Wait...Siren didn't actually answer my question. She never said if Beckett is alive or dead.

Beckett could be alive.

I snatch my wallet back up and race out of the hotel, back to the docks, and into a boat to search the water for him.

It takes me an hour of searching before I spot a man, gripping onto a piece of the boat floating in the water.

I kill the engine and pull him onto the boat with one hand. He collapses onto the floor of the boat. He coughs a few times, trying to rid his body of the saltwater. It brings back memories of before, of the last time I was in the water, and Siren saved my life.

"Who do you work for?" I ask, as I sit on a bench, waiting for him to compose himself. If I were smart or more weary, I would aim a gun at him until I got my answer. But I already suspect the truth. And he's in no condition to fight anyway.

He doesn't answer; he just coughs again. And I'm impatient.

"Do you work for Enzo Black?" I growl.

He smirks. "I work for the Black empire, yes. I'm Enzo's half brother, actually."

I exhale a deep breath, realizing that we are on the same side. And he almost killed me. He almost killed Siren, although she got her revenge for that.

"And who are you?" he asks.

"I'm Zeke Kane."

"Zeke Kane was supposed to be dead."

"I survived. I mean, Aria saved me."

"Is that why you work for her?"

"No, I work for her because I have to to protect the Black empire."

"Enzo and Kai are going to so happy to know you are alive. And Langston..."

My eyes water thinking about them. "They can't know. Not yet."

Beckett frowns, sitting up. "They have to know. They're still devastated by your death. They've been living with it for so long."

"And someday, I hope to be able to tell them I'm safe. But for now, they need to think I'm dead. It's the only way to protect them."

Beckett runs his hand through his hair.

"You have to pretend to be dead, too," I say.

He sighs. "Enzo's my half-brother. And I've learned to love Kai like a sister. I know they trust you. If you're telling me I need to pretend to be dead in order to keep them safe, then I will."

"Thank you," I nod, feeling the pain of not knowing what has happened to my friends and of making someone else they love pretend to be dead. To make them mourn another person they love.

He studies me a moment. "I don't understand your relationship with Aria. I don't know what you feel for her or if what I saw was all just an act on your part. But Aria tried to kill me. She knows who I am, that I work for the Black empire. You can't trust her; she's not on our side."

"Don't worry, I don't." I can never trust Siren, no matter how my heart aches to.

27

SIREN

THE NEXT MORNING IS EXHAUSTING, but not because of a lack of sleep. I slept hard with my best friend holding me, reminding me I have someone on my side.

The morning is exhausting because Zeke is completely ignoring me, while giving Nora his undivided attention. They both talk to each other like I'm not even here. In the hotel lobby, Zeke even offers to carry her bags.

I drive us to the airport, and the happy couple decide to sit in the back seat. Nora even rests her head on Zeke's chest.

So by the time we get to our plane, I'm exhausted from watching them together. I board the plane immediately, not speaking to either of them and taking a seat in the far back of the plane.

Nora boards next and looks over at me. "You okay?"

"Yep, just tired."

She nods and then heads to the cockpit.

Zeke boards last, carrying two coffees. He heads to the front and hands one to Nora, who takes it happily. And then he takes a seat across the aisle and ahead of me. He sips on his own coffee, continuing to ignore me.

Finally, we take off, and I try leaning my head back and sleeping. But Nora is back to her antics, and the plane dips side to side. This is her way of keeping us both awake and trying to force us to talk.

"Here," Zeke says, holding out the coffee cup to me.

"What are you doing?"

"Offering you a sip of my coffee. But it's my coffee, so don't drink it all. You are going to need to stay alert if we are going to survive this ride back."

I take the coffee and drink a couple of sips, accepting his peace offering before I return the cup.

"I would move back there to talk to you, but I'm afraid of getting tossed out a window with the way Nora is flying," Zeke says.

I don't laugh, but his comment earns him a smile.

"We need to talk," I say.

He frowns.

"Truth or sins?" I ask, hopeful that he'll play if he thinks there is a chance he'll get to fuck me on the plane.

"Who did you fuck to earn you a mile-high club membership?" he asks.

I smirk, I wasn't expecting that question. "Pete Miller."

"Pete Miller? That's such a boring name. And who was this Pete Miller? Someone you needed information from?"

His comment is like a jab to the heart.

"No, I fucked him because I wanted to. Because I thought it would be fun to have sex on a plane. And Pete was hot, despite having a boring name."

Zeke relaxes his shoulders.

"Is Beckett dead?" I ask, taking my own turn. I don't know if Zeke will tell me. He might take the easy way out and say sin; that way, he can pay me back for what I made him do last night and hide the truth about Beckett.

The sexual tension between us has heightened. All I want to do is to race over to Zeke and make him a member of the mile-high club too. If he chooses sin, then I'll get to. I need this.

But I also need his answer.

I wait for Zeke to make his decision. And the two choices flash before his eyes as well. He licks his lips, and I know what he's going to choose—sin. Even if it gets us both killed.

"Beckett's dead," he answers, surprising us both. He decides to give me what I need in order to tell Julian the truth, whether it is actually the truth or not.

28

———

ZEKE

WE LEFT Nora at the airport. She said she was meeting a friend in the Bahamas, but would check in on Siren soon. Siren and I headed straight to Julian's, both wanting credit for the first sin being over with.

We walk up the driveway to Julian's house. Siren doesn't bother knocking; she just walks in like this is her home. I guess it sort of is.

I follow behind. Siren seems to know exactly where Julian is, so I let her lead me through the house to a study. She's right, Julian is sitting in a lounge chair with a cigar in his mouth.

"I expected that task to be completed faster," Julian says with a grin.

We both ignore his remarks. Siren walks over to the bar cart in the corner and pours herself a drink. I decide to stay sober until I can celebrate my victory.

I take a seat in the remaining chair, and Siren leans against the wall with her drink in her hand.

"Is the job done?" Julian asks me.

"Yes. We found Eli Beckett."

Julian nods for me to continue as he puffs on his cigar.

"We found out he works for Mr. Black."

Julian grins, and I realize he already knew who Beckett worked for. This was a test to see what I would do.

"And we killed him," I finish.

Julian's eyebrows go up in surprise. It's then I realize the sins he will have me complete will be as devastating as the truths he wants me to spill. This time I got away easy. But next time? It could be a choice between killing two people I love, either physically or by spilling a truth.

"Interesting," Julian says, studying me closely, trying to determine if I'm telling the truth or lying. But then he turns his attention to Siren, not caring about my answer at all. He only cares about Siren's.

That's why he sent her with me—not to babysit. He knows I won't run as long as he threatens the lives of the people I love. He needs Siren to report to him if I completed the tasks or not. Because Siren can't lie, I can. And Julian knows that.

"Is Beckett dead?" Julian asks Siren.

Siren has been ignoring us so far, staring down at her drink. I have no idea what her answer will be. All I know is that to her, it will be the truth. But does she think Beckett is alive or dead? Or will she finally learn how to lie?

Her eyes flick up, somehow meeting both Julian's and my gaze at the same time.

"Yes, Eli Beckett is dead," she answers.

Julian grins. "Excellent." And then he turns to me. "Well done. I didn't think you had it in you."

"What's next?" I ask, anxious to get the five sins over with.

He puffs his cigar again. "Patience. I'll have a new game for you soon."

I stare at Julian in frustration. I want these stupid games of his over so I can go. But I also want to put off the next round as long as possible, because I'm not ready to go through that all over again so soon.

I stand up and leave, not sure if Siren is staying or coming. When I arrive at the truck, she hops into the passenger seat.

I drive us the minute up to my house and then kill the engine.

"Did you lie back there? To Julian?" I ask.

She opens her door, ignoring me. I follow, stomping after her into the house.

"Did you lie back there?" I ask again when we are both inside the house.

She spins around on her heels. "No, I told the truth as I know it."

I freeze. She truly thinks Beckett is dead. Or at least my lie let her believe that.

"I want you out of my house. I can't trust you," I say.

"It's really not up to you."

"You killed Beckett! A man who is on my side. A man who is loyal to my boss, to my friends."

She steps into my space. "No, I gave him a chance to live. A chance to save himself. If he's alive, it's because of me." She turns to walk away. But I grab her arm; she doesn't get to give a comment like that and then run off.

"What does that mean?"

"Nothing, I shouldn't have said anything."

"Siren, tell me."

"I warned him, okay? I warned him before the explosion happened."

Beckett didn't tell me the truth. He was just trying to convince me she isn't on our side. But what if she is?

It doesn't matter if she is or isn't, I still feel myself falling for her a little in this moment. A woman who is always selfish, always looking out for herself, did something to save a man she didn't even know when it could have cost her everything.

I want to tell her thank you for saving Beckett. For letting him live and making sure she only knew enough to be able to tell Julian she believes Beckett to be dead. But I can't thank her without telling her the truth that Beckett is alive, which would change her answer if Julian asks her again.

Instead, I do the only thing I can do. I fucking kiss her, giving her the biggest thank you I can offer without saying any words.

The kiss is more like a collision. We both need this kiss, while not wanting to admit it to the other. But as soon as our tongues meld, we lose all pretense of hating each other. My hand fists her hair; hers cling to my neck. Our bodies press together, and our tongues beg to move deeper into each other's mouths.

Siren claws at my shirt, and she shoves it up, needing to feel my chest. I stop the kiss long enough for her to get my shirt off. Then my lips cling to hers again, swearing silently that I will never let them go again.

I grab her shirt and pull it up before I realize I'll have to break the kiss again to remove her shirt.

I growl as I do.

This time, the moment our lips are apart is enough to remind me I don't just want to fuck her. I want answers. I need answers. I need to know whose side she is on. It's the only way to guard my heart. Even as it's already falling.

"Truth or sin?" I start.

"No." She grabs my neck and kisses me again. "We already played today."

She unhooks her bra as she continues to kiss me over my lips, then my jawline, then neck. It feels incredible, but it's not enough to fully distract me. Even when I take her breasts in my hands and hear her moans caress me.

"What is the vow you made to Julian?" I ask her.

She steps back. "I said not tonight."

I step forward. "I need the truth. I need to know whose side you are on. I need to know what keeps you from fighting back against Julian. What makes you save me?"

She opens her mouth, but I know it's to argue back, so I shut her up with a fierce kiss, slamming her into a wall of the hallway.

She shoves me back, refusing to let me deepen the kiss.

"Are you married to Julian?"

Her face falls, and I can't tell if it's truth or anger.

A buzz in her pocket breaks the moment.

"Don't answer it."

"I have to. It could be Julian." She grabs the phone from her pocket and answers. "Yes?"

I watch her eyes widen in fear, I watch the pulse in her neck speed, and her breath catch.

"I'll be right there," she finally says before ending the call.

I step in front of her. "You aren't going anywhere. Not without answering me."

"Let me go, Zeke."

"You aren't running to Julian because he called. Not without answering my questions first."

It's only then that I see the tears in her eyes. The way her hands tremble at her sides. She's scared to death. And I feel like a monster for blocking her path. Is she afraid Julian will punish her if she doesn't get to him quickly?

"I'll answer any damn question you have, but you have to let me go, now."

I pull my keys from my pocket and toss them to her. "Fine, but I'm going with you."

She nods, running toward my truck, picking up her trail of clothes along the way. I jump into the passenger seat, assuming we are headed to Julian's, but when we drive past his house, I'm utterly confused.

29

SIREN

I squeeze the steering wheel in a death grip as I drive down the road. Maybe I should have had Zeke drive? I'm too distracted. But I figure even my distracted driving is better than Zeke's best driving.

My thoughts are taken over by the phone call. I still can't believe what happened or that I feel it this harshly.

Julian always talks about there being consequences to my actions. If I break my vow, I will pay. But it's been years since he had to inflict any real consequence on me. And he's never inflicted a punishment this bad.

Bu then, I've never done anything this bad. I've never threatened Julian. Never hit him, never hurt him. I knew the moment I did that I crossed a line. And that eventually, Julian would make me pay for it.

I just thought him carving up my neck was the end of my retribution, that he had moved passed it.

Now I know he didn't.

But still, I didn't think it would torture this much. What Julian did shouldn't hurt me. It shouldn't affect me at all. But of course, it did. I'm human, after all. And you can't just turn off feelings, even if those emotions should be long gone.

Zeke studies me for a long time as I drive. He's still shirtless, but at least he's gripping his shirt in his hands so he can get dressed when we arrive.

I threw my shirt on in haste and didn't even bother to put my bra back on. I'm sure Zeke can see my nipples still hard beneath my shirt.

Zeke's hand reaches out, flicking on the radio. I don't pay him any attention. I'm surprised he turned the radio on at all. He usually prefers the silence.

But then I hear him sing. It's horrible. His voice is way off-key.

I bite back a smile. "Your voice is horrible."

"Well, sorry we can't all be pros like you."

He continues singing, and my smile brightens, the ache in my chest getting just bearable enough for me to drive.

And then I find myself humming along to the song too. My right hand loosens on the steering wheel, falling to the side. Our hands find each other. And when Zeke's fingers lock with mine, I feel him take on some of my pain, even though he doesn't know why I'm in such a state.

He doesn't know any of the words, but he keeps singing along. I finally join him when it returns to the chorus of a new Miley Cyrus song I've never heard before. But it feels fitting. The song talks about telling a guy to slide away back to the ocean. And it's the exact words I want to repeat to too many men in my life—all for very different reasons.

30

ZEKE

Siren stops the car in front of the hospital.

My heart stops.

"Nora?" I ask, assuming she got into an accident. It's the only person I know of in Siren's life that would cause the pain I feel drumming through her body.

She shakes her head. And I exhale in relief for myself and Siren.

"A family member?" I ask, realizing I don't know any of Siren's family, or if any of them are alive.

"No."

She steps out of the truck, and I follow.

I link our fingers again as we walk inside, ready to face whatever heartbreak awaits us as a team.

Siren takes a deep breath and then walks up to the front desk with me still holding onto her. I grip her hand in comfort as much as for me as for her.

"I'm here to see Hugo Martinez."

I frown. *Martinez? That's her last name. But I thought she said it wasn't a family member?*

The nurse smiles sadly at the mention of the man's

name. He must be in critical condition for her to give us that sort of response. "Are you a family member?"

My eyes go to Siren's, not sure how she's going to respond. She can't lie, and I'm sure only family members will be allowed to see him.

She closes her eyes for a second, as if this entire situation is painful.

I give her hand a tight squeeze, reassuring her. Even if the nurse won't let us back because we aren't immediate family, I will find a way for her to see Hugo if he means so much to her.

Siren opens her eyes, ignoring me, and says, "I'm his wife."

I forget everything after those words. I forget the look on Siren's face. I forget what the nurse said. I forget how it felt when Siren slipped out of my hand and walked away without me, leaving me rooted to my spot in the waiting room.

And now, I have no idea how long I've been standing here, just that I have been waiting. Waiting to understand how it's possible. Waiting to find out what this means. *Why this man, who Siren says is her husband, in the hospital? Why?*

I pace while I wait, coming up with a hundred different answers, and none of them make sense in my head.

Until I see her—Siren Aria Torres Martinez. So many names and none of them make sense to me.

"How is your dear hubby?" I ask, not hiding the anger in my voice now that she's returned to the waiting room.

She holds out a styrofoam cup of coffee to me. "I got you this."

I laugh. "Is that supposed to make up for you lying to me?"

"I didn't lie."

"Really? Because I seem to remember you saying you weren't married."

She takes a step toward me. "I never said I wasn't married. I held up my ringless finger and implied it. But I never said I wasn't."

She's right, of course. She never actually said she wasn't married.

I run my hand through my hair as I finally sink into a chair. "Is he going to be okay?"

She sits next to me, still gripping the cup of coffee. "I think so. He's in critical condition after a car accident."

My anger takes hold of me again, and I stand up suddenly. "You're married, and you still fucked me!"

"It's not that simple."

"It sure as hell is that simple to me! You are married! You're a cheating whore!"

She stands up. "Call me whatever will make you feel better, but it's not true. Being married is more than just a signature on a legal piece of paper."

"So, you don't love Hugo Martinez?"

She doesn't answer. Because she loves him.

I slump back into the chair. "Explain. Now."

"I met Hugo when I was eighteen. He saved my life. Saved me from going down a path where I would have ended up dead in a ditch somewhere. We fell in love and got married.

"A few years later, Hugo needed saving. And it was my turn to save him. He got mixed up with a drug lord. He owed him a lot of money that he could never pay back.

"I tried everything. I gave the drug lord all the money I had. I sold every possession I owned. It wasn't enough. I even offered my body to him, but he would only take money. So I snuck into Julian Reed's house to try to steal something I could sell. He caught me and offered me a deal."

She takes a deep breath, and I'm entranced by her strength even if I hate her right now.

"So, I made a vow to Julian to save Hugo's life."

I narrow my eyes.

"Julian paid the drug lord and freed Hugo. I paid Julian back with the only thing he wanted—my loyalty. I vowed to work for him for ten years. To never lay a hand on Julian. To never disobey him. To follow his orders. And for the last seven years, I've been doing just that. But then I threatened Julian, so he arranged a car accident to show me what happens when I break my vow to him."

There's more. As painful as her story already is, I know there is more.

"I made a vow to two men. I vowed ten years of service to Julian. And I vowed my heart to Hugo. But Hugo betrayed me. We've been separated since, but never got around to filing for divorce."

"It's why you don't like people saving you; you don't like owing others anything. They can't betray you that way."

She nods. "Yes. I've been branded by three men. Saved and protected by all. But in the end, they all eventually hurt me."

Except me, I haven't yet. But I'm about to.

"Do you still love Hugo? Even though he hurt you? Even though you are no longer faithful to that marriage?"

She stares down at the cup. "I shouldn't. He doesn't love me. But I'm not sure you just let go of love like that. I wish I could because then maybe I could end my vow to Julian. Even though Hugo betrayed me, I'm still loyal to Julian. I still do everything to keep Hugo safe and protected. I can't let Julian hurt him. If you call that love, then that is what it is. But it feels like Hugo stole a piece of my heart I don't know how to get back."

I understand the feeling. Because right now, as much as I hate Siren, she stole a piece of my heart. Even now, watching her in pain, I feel myself falling for her again. But she's not mine to fall for. She never will be. She'll always choose Hugo or Julian. She doesn't have a choice. And if she ever gets free of those two men, she has no reason to fall for me. She will protect her heart no matter what—it's already cost her too much.

I stand up, knowing where Siren stands in my heart, but not being able to accept it.

"Zeke," she starts, but she never finishes her sentence.

"It's my turn to make a vow."

She sits up taller, and I can see fear in her eyes as she waits.

"I vow to never save you again, Siren. From now on, I'm only saving myself."

And then I turn and walk away, intending to be true to my word.

But is it too late to keep that vow when my heart is already falling?

The End

Thank you so much for reading! Zeke and Siren's story continues in Reckless Fall #3

Grab the entire Sinful Truths series below!
Sinful Truth #1
Twisted Vow #2
Reckless Fall #3
Tangled Promise #4
Fallen Love #5
Broken Anchor #6

Read Enzo and Kai's story below in the Truth or Lies series!
(You also get to read Zeke's beginning)
Taken by Lies #1
Betrayed by Truths #2
Trapped by Lies #3
Stolen by Truths #4
Possessed by Lies #5
Consumed by Truths #6

FREE BOOKS

Read **Not Sorry** for **FREE**! And sign up to get my latest releases & updates here→EllaMiles.com/freebooks

Follow me on BookBub to get notified of my new releases→Follow on BookBub Here

Join Ella's Bellas FB group to grab my **FREE** book **Pretend I'm Yours**→Join Ella's Bellas Here

ORDER SIGNED PAPERBACKS

I love putting my signed paperbacks on SALE!

Check them out by visiting my website:
https://ellamiles.com/signed-paperbacks

ALSO BY ELLA MILES

SINFUL TRUTHS:

Sinful Truth #1

Twisted Vow #2

Reckless Fall #3

Tangled Promise #4

Fallen Love #5

Broken Anchor #6

TRUTH OR LIES:

Taken by Lies #1

Betrayed by Truths #2

Trapped by Lies #3

Stolen by Truths #4

Possessed by Lies #5

Consumed by Truths #6

DIRTY SERIES:

Dirty Beginning

Dirty Obsession

Dirty Addiction

Dirty Revenge

Dirty: The Complete Series

ALIGNED SERIES:

Aligned: Volume 1 (Free Series Starter)

Aligned: Volume 2

Aligned: Volume 3

Aligned: Volume 4

Aligned: The Complete Series Boxset

UNFORGIVABLE SERIES:

Heart of a Thief

Heart of a Liar

Heart of a Prick

Unforgivable: The Complete Series Boxset

MAYBE, DEFINITELY SERIES:

Maybe Yes

Maybe Never

Maybe Always

Definitely Yes

Definitely No

Definitely Forever

STANDALONES:

Pretend I'm Yours

Finding Perfect

Savage Love

Too Much

Not Sorry

ABOUT THE AUTHOR

Ella Miles writes steamy romance, including everything from dark suspense romance that will leave you on the edge of your seat to contemporary romance that will leave you laughing out loud or crying. Most importantly, she wants you to feel everything her characters feel as you read.

Ella is currently living her own happily ever after near the Rocky Mountains with her high school sweetheart husband. Her heart is also taken by her goofy five year old black lab who is scared of everything, including her own shadow.

Ella is a USA Today Bestselling Author & Top 50 Bestselling Author.

Stalk Ella at:
www.ellamiles.com
ella@ellamiles.com